THE BEST OF THE BEST
THE FIGHTING
5TH MARINES VIETNAM
DYING DELTA

To Harry D. Penny Jr.,
Thank you for your service both as a Corpsman and in Law Enforcement.
Semper Fi
Paul A. McNally

PAUL A. MCNALLY

Outskirts Press, Inc.
Denver, Colorado

The opinions expressed in this manuscript are solely the opinions of the author and do not represent the opinions or thoughts of the publisher. The author has represented and warranted full ownership and/or legal right to publish all the materials in this book.

The Best Of The Best The Fighting 5th Marines Vietnam
Dying Delta
All Rights Reserved.
Copyright © 2009 Paul A. McNally
V5.0

This book may not be reproduced, transmitted, or stored in whole or in part by any means, including graphic, electronic, or mechanical without the express written consent of the publisher except in the case of brief quotations embodied in critical articles and reviews.

Outskirts Press, Inc.
http://www.outskirtspress.com

ISBN: 978-1-4327-2609-6

Library of Congress Control Number: 2008933545

Outskirts Press and the "OP" logo are trademarks belonging to Outskirts Press, Inc.

PRINTED IN THE UNITED STATES OF AMERICA

TABLE OF CONTENTS

Acknowledgments	vii
Introduction	xi
Chapter 1: The Interview	1
Chapter 2: Childhood	3
Chapter 3: The Greenbelt	9
Chapter 4: Smigel's Corner	15
Chapter 5: You never Know	19
Chapter 6: Pure Stupidity	21
Chapter 7: Joining The Marine Corps	23
Chapter 8: Boot Camp	27
Chapter 9: Rifle Range	31
Chapter 10: Graduation	37
Chapter 11: Camp Geiger	39
Chapter 12: Camp Lejeune	43
Chapter 13: Med – Cruise	45
Chapter 14: Back to Camp Lejeune- For New Orders	51
Chapter 15: Cruise Ship To Vietnam	53
Chapter 16: Okinawa	57
Chapter 17: Arrival in Vietnam	59
Chapter 18: Liberty Lives	65

Chapter 19: Running Point	69
Chapter 20: Tet – 1967	71
Chapter 21: First Combat	73
Chapter 22: Tunnel Rat	77
Chapter 23: R&R	81
Chapter 24: Mess Duty	83
Chapter 25: Guard Duty – Chu Lia	87
Chapter 26: Shit Bird	91
Chapter 27: Leaving Chu Lia	93
Chapter 28: The Move Up North	99
Chapter 29: Operation Union	103
Chapter 30: Mail Call	109
Chapter 31: May 12, 1967	119
Chapter 32: FNG's	133
Chapter 33: Operation Union II	141
Chapter 34: Dying Delta	155
Chapter 35: Going Home	159
Chapter 36: Recuperation	163
Chapter 37: Discharged	173
Chapter 38: Silver Star	175
Chapter 39: Reality	179
Chapter 40: Last Duty Station	183
Chapter 41: Party Time	187
Chapter 42: Potomac River Incident	193
Chapter 43: End of my tour	195
Chapter 44: Civilian Again	197
Chapter 45: Wonderful Mary	199

Chapter 46: Woodstock	203
Chapter 47: Lincoln Prep	207
Chapter 48: California here I come	209
Chapter 49: Learning the Carpentry & Leather Trades	211
Chapter 50: Janet	213
Chapter 51: Starting College	215
Chapter 52: Main Campus	217
Chapter 53: Debbie	219
Chapter 54: Gainesville Florida	221
Chapter 55: The Butler Family	223
Chapter 56: Santa Fe Community College	225
Chapter 57: Pittsburgh	227
Chapter 58: Back to Gainesville	229
Chapter 59: Constant Reminder	231
Chapter 60: DVOP	233
Chapter 61: USPS	235
Chapter 62: Karen – My Life Partner	237
Chapter 63: Summarization	243
Index	245

ACKNOWLEDGMENTS

It seems to me that it has been a long road traveled since 1983 when I first started writing about my time spent in Vietnam. At first, all I wanted to do was get down on paper what I remembered of my time spent there, while it was still very vivid in my mind. With encouragement from a few friends, I took the first step to make something more of what I had written. Patience, a good friend of the Vet organization I was a member of in the late 1970's early 80's was one of those friends who did the first critiques of my work. Patience was married to Robert C. Mason, the author of [CHICKENHAWK], a great book about the helicopter pilots who flew them in Vietnam. With Patience's help and encouragement, I began the long process of learning how to take what I had been writing and turn it into something worthwhile to read. I can never thank you enough for your inspiration.

The first publication of my work, [Coming of Age] came about when two very old friends of mine, Wendy and Ken, created a literary magazine called the [LABYRINTH] in the winter of 1988. Because of their time constraints and schedule issues and money, they published the fourth and last issue of Labyrinth in 1990, with my story ending in the early stages of Operation Union. Thanks Wendy for helping make my dream come true.

It wasn't until 2004 that I had another chance to publish my work, when the 1st Marine Division Association was looking for new stories and photographs for Volume III of Vietnam. I sent them a story that covered both Operation Union and Union II called [A Grunt's Point Of View]. I was finally working on a computer by then and all I'll say about that is, thank God that he let someone create Word Perfect and its predecessors; it has made writing for me so more enjoyable.

Not long after that time, my lovely niece Olivia asked me 47 questions about Vietnam that were for her high school project, which in turn made me want to put all the elements of this story together. Thanks go to you Olivia for asking me to do your interview and to your teacher for coming up with that project.

About this time I started meeting people on my new mail route who wanted to help me on my mission. Mrs. Sapp was the first to offer help in editing and direction of the book and her suggestions strongly set the course of it.

Then Mrs. Karen, a published author of numerous books - sold in Europe –did some editing and gave me much encouragement to continue on.

I found out that Wendy and her friends had created a writers workshop at a local bookstore and after several critiques of my work, I learned more of what I needed to do to improve my work. My thanks and gratitude goes to all you folks at the bookstore.

During the same time I was going to these workshops, I met another person on my mail route, Dr. John Price – a retired professor of literature from the University of Florida. Dr. Price was also retired from the Army, starting out as private in the beginning of WW II and then spending the following 37 years either active or in the Reserves, obtaining the rank of Colonel. All I can say is this book would not be what it is if not for Dr. Price. I cannot thank you enough, Sir, for all of your great help and advice you have offered me.

Nearing the conclusion of what I hoped was the final

revision of the story another one of my patrons on my mail route, Dr. David Wahl, heard about it and asked if he could read it. Thanks to Dr. Wahl, this material is now suitable for you and most anybody else to read. Thanks Doc for your great insight.

Along with my brother Mike and my wife Karen, there were many more of my friends that had a hand, one way or another, in helping me in the completion of this story.

Gary L. Tornes, author of [Apprentices of War] who has been a very old friend of my brother Mike and a new one of mine is one of these people. Gary, a fellow Marine Corps Vietnam veteran, also from the enlisted ranks, wrote his memoir of his time spent there. After he read a draft of my story and I his story, we both realized that we had uncanny parallels happen in our lives during and after our time in Vietnam. Thank you all for your time, honesty, and encouragement.

Last, but very far from least, my benefactors and friends, Mrs. Ruth Parker Dunavant, and Mrs. June Kent, both of you have been wonderful and insightful people being the sounding board for me of my successes and tribulations on this journey.

I thank you all from the bottom of my heart for helping me complete this story and bring it to publication; I couldn't have done it if it weren't for all of you.

INTRODUCTION

In the beginning of the year 1983 while working in the DVOP [Disabled Veterans Outreach Program], I felt a strong imperative to recall my time in Vietnam and transcribe what I had remembered on to paper.

In the long run while going through this process, I found out that there were other people besides me that were interested in what I had written. Over time, I learned how to turn this material into a true memoir of my life, and by doing so learned to put into perspective how it all affected what I do in every day life, past and present.

Most of what I had written is mainly based on how I recalled it, and is not meant to be a chronologically accurate history of Delta Company, 5th Marines, 1st Marine Division from 1966 and 1967. Though most of what I had written is based on accurate history depicted in the book [A few Good Men] by Ronald J. Brown, and many of the names of people I mention in this story are accurate; some may not be due to the time passed before I began this project.

This story is dedicated to the true hero's of Vietnam War, the ones who gave it their all, the ones whose names are on the "WALL."

CHAPTER 1
THE INTERVIEW

Olivia, my dear niece, when you tried to interview me about my experiences in wartime Vietnam, I was reluctant to talk, as many veterans are. This long letter is an attempt to answer your questions. My purpose is threefold: [1] To set down a straightforward account to satisfy the curiosity and at the same time to add something to our family history; [2] To tell the general public exactly what things were like in Vietnam – lessons to be learned; [3] To help restore my mental equilibrium by getting it all on paper, where in my conscious mind, I learned a more effective way of dealing with the horrors of war I had experienced – an experiment in therapy for Post Traumatic Stress Disorder [PTSD].

This letter tells the story of my life in the Marine Corps: why I volunteered, my training, combat in Vietnam, how I got two Purple Hearts and a Silver Star, my lengthy postwar rehabilitation. Though my time in the Marine Corps began over forty years ago, the lessons learned are relevant to today's conflicts in the Middle East.

Again we find our country involved in a war similar in many ways to the one I fought in Vietnam from October 1966 to June 2, 1967. Unfortunately, just as we did in the Vietnam War, I believe we are making similar mistakes in strategy while fighting the war in Iraq and possibly also in Afghanistan. To learn more about the strategy of fighting a war, read [ON Strategy] by Harry G Summers Jr. You can find it online at Amazon.com.

I began writing this letter or memoir of my time spent in the M.C. [Marine Corps] and, primarily, about my time served in Vietnam beginning in 1983, while I was working with disabled veterans in the VA hospitable. I took participation in group discussions with patients suffering from PTSD. We sat around a big table and recounted our wartime experiences in the hope of restoring our mental health. After one of these meetings, it dawned on me to put my nightmare-causing experiences down on paper to exorcise my demons. By this means, Olivia, I learned how to answer your questions; and this turned out to be an effective way for me to cope with my postwar problems. As soon as I was sure of the curative powers of writing, I presented my idea to the PTSD director and he had it incorporated into the program.

One of the first questions you asked me was: "Why did I join the M.C.?" In order to answer that question, I will give you an overview of my life from the time I was born until I actually joined the M.C., on through the time I spent in it. This will give you a much more insightful and thorough answer to that question and most of the other questions you had in mind.

CHAPTER 2
CHILDHOOD

The month of February 1947 had one of the worst winter storms of the Twentieth Century hit Philadelphia, Pennsylvania. Over 20 inches of snow fell in 24 hours, bringing the city to a near standstill. It was during this storm my mother went into labor. My father had a very difficult time getting my mother to the hospital so she could deliver me. Three days later my father was finally able to get back to the hospital to see his new baby.

As a child, I grew up in Cheltenham Township, a suburb just northwest of the city; and over the years, nine children would be born to complete our family. Jack was the oldest; Mike next; then me; then Tom; the first of the girls, Liz and Sue; twin boys, Jim and Steve-and finally your mother and my youngest sister, Meg. Our father was a medical doctor with over thirty years in general practice and nearly six more years - solely in obstetrics. After working over 36 years as a physician, he should have been ready, one might think, for retirement. Not so. For a year, after he closed down his practice, he took off from work to do nothing but study for the exam he would have to take if he wanted to practice medicine in the State of Florida. He passed the test and for many more years afterward, worked in his profession before completely retiring. He died just short of his 92nd birthday.

Mother was a registered nurse when she married my

father, but soon became a mother and full-time housewife, bridge player and golfer. As a father myself of a 26 year-old son, I have often wondered how she managed to raise all of us without going a little nuts over the years. In my case, I, more so than any of my siblings, probably had more to do with causing my mother's hair to rapidly start turning gray back then.

I can only imagine what my mother thought when she found out about one of my first episodes of going out to deal with the world. My brother, Jack, the historian of the family, told me about an incident that happened when I was nearly five years old.

I decided to explore the surrounding neighborhood, taking my younger brother, Tom, along with me on my journey. We were all at my grandmother's house and my brother, Jack, was watching over us while my parents were across the street visiting my Aunt Tilley. Somehow, I managed to get outside with Tom in tow and got three blocks from the house and was trying to cross a very busy Germantown Avenue. We were as naked as the day we were born and there was snow on the ground. Our guardian angel that day came in the form of a city construction worker who saw Tom and me trying to cross the avenue. He stopped us and marched us back to our grandmother's house. Jack told me that when he answered the door and saw this very big black man standing there with Tom and me standing behind him in the nude, it scared the crap out of him.

Another example would be the next year when I was at summer camp and discovered a yellow jacket nest in the ground. There were plenty of these insects coming and going from their home. This was the first time I had seen one and I guess my natural curiosity got the best of me. I made the stupid mistake of poking a stick down the entrance. This blunder would be my first brush with death. I most likely would have died had I not dived into a pond that was about 100 yards from where hundreds of the yellow jackets started their attack. Even that escape measure didn't prevent me from going into a coma for three days. The one thing that I still see vividly in my mind's eye is that during the coma, I was falling, or more like floating, through this giant vortex made of huge honeycombs. Years later a psychologist told me "If I had hit the bottom of that vortex, I most likely would have died." My parents were in Europe on vacation when this happened; I can only imagine what their reactions were when they got the news of this incident.

Then there was the time I played hooky on the last day of school in second grade. I brought my brother, Tom, along with me. My brother and I were walking to St. Joseph's grade school and were passing by Billy Broken Arms house, which butted up to the township's greenbelt. Billy saw us and came over and started talking to us, saying things like how nice a day it was and that we should be outside enjoying it. Billy Broken Arm was about four years older than I, he broke his arm the year before and had a cast on it; thus, the nickname. Since it was the last day of school, I agreed we could skip it and not get into any trouble. I could not have been more wrong. The school got in touch with my mother about our absence and once she realized that we were missing, all of the agencies in Cheltenham went into a search mode. An hour or so later, after skipping school, I noticed a lot of adults getting into a line to comb through the greenbelt. With my brother in tow, I searched for a good hiding place and found one nearby inside an old burned-out hollow tree that was still standing.

Yelling out our names, the search party walked right past us. I made sure Tom didn't give us away by putting one hand over his mouth while at the same time giving him the sign with the other to keep quiet, for some reason I did not want to be found by these people. My older brother

Mike was the one who found us. I guess he remembered the time I was talking about that tree when we were eating dinner one night. Mike marched us back to the school and at first everyone seemed relieved and happy that we weren't kidnapped or harmed. But a lesson had to be taught to us for our actions that day. The nuns got the first crack when they took out a clear one-gallon glass jar that was full of some very disgusting slop and did a very good job of making us believe we were going to have to consume its contents. As bad as that seemed to us, the clincher happened when this huge black cop came in and put us into handcuffs and then into his patrol car. He put the fear of God into us when he started driving away, telling us that we were going to jail. After a ton of tears and our pleading for mercy, he told us that he would release us if we promised never to do what we did ever again. We sincerely promised and neither of us pulled off such a stunt throughout the remainder of our grade school years. By the time our mother and father were finished disciplining us you can take it for granted that we didn't even think of doing something like that again.

I went through second grade twice. The first time was when I went to Melrose Academy-a Catholic grade school. I had started this school in kindergarten and was considered a normal student until I got to second grade and had Sister Nalla as my teacher. This nun was very large in stature and a no-nonsense authoritarian. I was never sure why this nun had it in for me, but possibly I may have had ADD [Attention Deficit Disorder]-something that wasn't recognized or treated back then. Whatever it was, I truly feared going to her class. One of her favorite methods of discipline was grabbing my left wrist with her left hand and swinging me around in a circle counter-clockwise till I became airborne. Once she got me in the right orbit she would start whacking my rear end with a half-inch thick yardstick. This kind of treatment may have been the reason that I was absent for more than half that year due to illness. My father had my tonsils removed later that same year and that may be the reason I became a very healthy kid once I was out of that woman's class.

CHAPTER 3
THE GREENBELT

Throughout my childhood, I would love to bring home all kinds of critters that I would find down the street in the greenbelt that ran through the township. My mother was usually the first person in our household to see what I brought home and was the judge and jury on whether or not I got to keep it. She wasn't very fond of the many different snakes I loved catching to bring back to try scaring my sisters. I was very fortunate in that a Naturalist lived down the street from our house and I was included in his field trips into the greenbelt, along with some of the other neighborhood kids. He was the person who taught me how to recognize every living thing in that greenbelt. By the time I was seven years old, I could recognize all the poisonous snakes roaming in that part of the state. The ones I brought home were all harmless.

My mother did put her foot down when I brought home a 25-pound Alligator-Snapping Turtle that someone brought back from the Deep South and released into the greenbelt. Mom wouldn't let me keep it, so I released it in a swampy area where I thought it would have a better chance of surviving. Throughout the next five years, I would often get to see it in that same area until one day I found it dead with its shell smashed. From all the different sneaker footprints that I found around the turtle, I figured that it was most likely done by a group of local out-of-control teenagers. I think it must be a primal instinct that causes a person, who by himself would not have killed this wonderful creature-but, with a group of his peers, goes into a pack mode and kills first and asks questions later. When will it all stop, or even better, when will the youth and their leaders on this planet learn to abandon the pack mentality and learn to enjoy and embrace the diversity of everything on this planet? Who knows, it could save many lives some day.

I was about six when I met the Naturalist who lived down the street from our home and was fascinated by all the things he taught us on our field trips into the greenbelt. I will always be grateful to the founding fathers of Cheltenham for allowing the creation of that greenbelt, for I spent most of my free time playing and learning in them.

When I was about ten years old, I realized there was money to be made in the woods. My first business venture, with the help of my father's finances, was trapping muskrats-whose pelts I would sell to Sears and Roebuck for an average of $1.25 per pelt. I learned some important business knowledge along with the importance of conservation of wildlife after the year I spent at this. First, it doesn't take long to nearly wipe out the source of your income [the muskrats]. Second, the amount of time I was investing [trapping, skinning, tanning, and transporting the finished product, along with lost or stolen traps] added up to a net loss instead of a gain.

By the time I was in my teens, I can honestly say that I felt like I was part of the greenbelts, I knew every last inch of them and you could say that they were my best friend and teacher. I was not a loner that spent all my time in the woods, for I had friends who would join me on many of my journeys. We would build tree forts or underground forts, or spend hours playing cowboys and Indians. As we got older, we played war games that morphed into some serious business. Our weapons by then had escalated to BB-guns, slingshots and cherry bombs. It was amazing that none of us was seriously injured. Unbeknownst to me at the time, it was the playing of these kinds of games that would give me a bit of an advantage when it became no longer a game in Vietnam.

One of my best friends was Gerry Doyle, God bless his departed soul, whom I had known since I started going to school at St. Joseph's. All through grade school we were pretty inseparable and did a lot of crazy things together, topping the list was the time Hurricane Hazel approached Pennsylvania. In a construction dumpsite that was across Tookany Creek Parkway we found some old truck inner tubes that we patched up and some discarded plywood that we secured to the inner tubes to create a raft. Our plan was to take this raft and ride it down the normally placid Tookany Creek when it flooded from the approaching storm. The creek was about 40-50 feet wide and about 2 feet deep on average when it wasn't flooded. From past experience, we knew that the creek would get over triple that size when it flooded. When the hurricane rains hit our area, the creek turned into a white-water enthusiast's dream. Gerry and I launched our raft into these waters and rode the raft for more than three miles. From the launch till the end of the trip, both Gerry and I were letting out loud screams while we were exchanging looks of disbelief as we rode our raft down this creek. We were having the time of our lives until we started coming up to a bend in the creek. We both knew that there was a 20-foot diameter flood drainage tube just around this bend and when we started to hear the tremendous roar caused from the surge of water blasting from the tube, we started to get a bit nervous. Luckily, as we approached this bend, we were able to maneuver the raft close enough to the bank to get safely back on land. It was a good thing we were able to get off our raft, because it was basically vaporized when it hit the solid stream of water that was shooting some 50 feet straight out into the flooded creek. I'm sure both of us would have encountered similar results had we stayed on it.

You name any sport and I probably played it, some longer than others. I was usually one of the last persons picked when we played games during recess throughout grade school, mainly because of my small stature compared to my classmates. It was in the sports that weren't played in grade school that I mostly excelled. I sometimes think I may have been a reincarnated fish. My mother often told me that I seemed more at home in the water than I was on land. From the age of six, I competed in swimming matches and from the age of twelve in diving matches until I joined the M.C. When I was 13 years old, I played on a 105-pound football team when I weighed in at whopping 85-pounds and played on both the offensive and defensive teams in the guard position. I received the most valuable player trophy after my first and last year playing that game.

I've always loved the challenge sports provided. I started playing golf at the age of eleven on Caddie's Day. Every Monday, Melrose Country Club would close the golf course so the ground crews could go out in force and spruce it up. This was the same day that anybody who caddied there could go out and play a round for free. Caddying was the first job I had working for someone else. I played every Monday with my newfound friends and coworkers. I actually did caddie on occasion, mostly for women golfers who used smaller, lighter golf-bags compared to what the men usually had. When we were sitting around waiting on work, card games were the norm and I probably made more money playing cards than caddying. I still play golf at least once a week.

The township greenbelt butted into the city's greenbelt called Tookany Creek Park. If you followed the city greenbelt to the east, you would pass by the back yard of our home. If you crossed the parkway that ran by my backyard, on into the park, you would find the discharge exit of one of the main flood systems that came out of the township.

The second house we occupied in Cheltenham was in one of the lowest parts of the township and because it was, a flood discharge system was built into all the streets of that section to discharge any heavy rainwater past that area into the city greenbelt. It wasn't very long after I discovered this system that I could go into it and come out in any part of Cheltenham it serviced. What I didn't realize back then was the fact that once again I was training for my future. I had no idea that walking and crawling through the tunnels would be highly useful to me as a Marine in Vietnam, where one of my most dangerous experiences came while I was in a tunnel. The name given to the people who did this job in Vietnam was "Tunnel Rat", a nickname I took pride in being called.

CHAPTER 4
SMIGEL'S CORNER

When I was nearly fourteen years old, I started to venture out of the greenbelts and into the city where a lot of my caddie friends lived. I started to hang out with my cousin Mike and his friends at Smigel's Corner, which was located in a section of the city called Lansdale. This corner gang was just one of many such groups throughout the city and the ones in the Lansdale area were all part of the A&C Gang, which represented over 1500 members. This was a sizeable group who were capable of forming in a very short notice if so needed. The Marine Corps got and still does get a lot of their recruits from these corner gangs and Smigel's Corner supplied six of them beginning in 1964.

When summer vacation started when I was sixteen, I made up a story to tell my parents about having a part-time job and a place to stay down in Wildwood, New Jersey. In actuality, my cousin Mike, Bill [a funny member of the Smigel's Corner gang] and I shared the attic of a hotel that was managed by the parents of another member of our group. We got this place only after we were discovered living under the same hotel. We figured we would find employment and a place to live once we got there, but until we did, we would sleep under the hotel on its floor of sand. About the third or fourth night there, I was up on the boardwalk panhandling and trying to meet some girls. After not succeeding very well in either, I decided to call it a night and head on back to my bed of sand. As I was crawling under the hotel in the dark making my way to where I was sleeping, I came across what I thought was a piece of bamboo lying in the sand. Thinking I could use it to hang the new sweater that I was wearing on it, I brought it along. After I got to my sleeping quarters, I started trying to push it into the sand. I was leaning over it, putting all my weight on it when it broke. It turned out not to be a piece of bamboo but a piece of neon light made to look like bamboo. On the first break, I fell into it, with the sharp edge of it slicing my upper lip in half. It hit my teeth causing it to break again, with me falling further onto the piece sticking out of the sand. That piece went into the front part of my left shoulder. To say I was bleeding profusely would be an understatement. It must have scared the hell out of the couple managing the hotel when I banged on their door and they opened it up to see me all covered in blood. All I remember after that was waking up in a hospital the next day with my father by my bed, smiling. Two weeks later, after the stitches were out, I was back down at Wildwood, this time with a place to stay up in the attic of the hotel and a kind of a part-time job working in a parking lot, mainly for tips when I would bring the car up for the owner. It was a great way to meet the chicks and that's how I met Roxanne from Cherry Hill, New Jersey. Ah, to be sixteen again. That summer was the year I lost my virginity; and goes down as one of the most X-rated ones in my memory and I'll just leave it at that. Ah, the memories.

Our living quarters up in the attic of the hotel were sparse to say the least, but because we lived there for nothing it was bearable except when it came to Bill. It's possible that because his sneakers smelled so badly and because they skunked-up the whole attic, they very well could have been used as lethal weapons somewhere else. Once it was realized that his sneakers were the source of this horrible order, Bill was given an ultimatum, and that was, "Anytime you have your sneakers off up in the attic, they had better be out on the window stile, with the window closed." One night cousin Mike and I came back to the attic only to be greeted with the undeniable terrible smell of Bill's sneakers. Bill had been warned. All he got done before he passed-out from one to many beers - yes, even back in 1962, it was easy for us to acquire beer - was to take off his sneakers and let them drop at the foot of his cot before he passed-out. To teach Bill that we weren't messing around when it came to his sneakers, we decided to fight odor with odor. First we got his after-shave lotion and emptied the contents of it equally into each of his shoes. Next we took his peanut butter and filled-up both shoes with it. Believe it or not, after Bill cleaned out the peanut butter from his shoes, the odor was gone.

CHAPTER 5
YOU NEVER KNOW

F ate was on my side again when on the last day of that summer I hitched-hiked back to Philadelphia to the old corner, just missing some of the guys who had driven off. Since no one else was around, I decided to walk home. On my way, I heard a horrendous crash on the block I had just passed. I went back to find the guys I just missed in a terrible accident. Butch, who owned 1955 Oldsmobile convertible, just had an argument with his girl friend and was angry. He was doing 90 miles an hour down a residential street.

Butch was one of the older guys that hung-out on Smigel's corner. He was one of the first guys to get a driver license, and a car to drive. A lady, who was pulling into the intersection in front of him, froze when she saw him coming. Butch tried to go around her only to smash head first into a large oak tree. He hit the tree with such force that the headlights of the car were only inches from touching each other on the other side of the tree. How they survived is beyond me. It took the emergency people over an hour to extract Butch from under the dashboard. He received a concussion and compound fractures to both legs and feet, but recovered nicely. Bill, who was up front riding shotgun - who went on to become Army Vietnam Vet - was a very muscular short man who worked in the tree cutting business - came out of the accident with just a big bump on his forehead and a very bruised chest - whose imprint was imbedded in the dashboard several inches deep. Bill died several years later, but not from what the accident did to him. He died from what the exposure to "Agent Orange" in Vietnam did to him. Russ was in the back seat; drivers side and put his feet up on the back of the seat in front of him. He later told me that doing that was probably the reason he broke his back, putting him in a back brace for over a year, which afterwards, he seemed OK. Chris, who was at least six-feet tall, was next to Russ; the convertible top that was down came up and the frame of it hit him in the head, giving him a concussion. At the same time, his long legs went under the seat in front of him, causing compound fractures to both of his thighbones, requiring pins to be inserted into both legs. Had I got back twenty minutes sooner, I can only wonder at what would have happened. I had a feeling that my Guardian Angel may have had something to do with that and also later on in Vietnam, keeping me out of harms way.

CHAPTER 6
PURE STUPIDITY

That car crash is a prime example of the dumb things people who were involved with corner gangs seemed to get into. Unfortunately, I was not immune to this stupidity. Every year during the Halloween season, we played a game of "Who can steal the most pumpkins?" To play the game, you first had to ante-up $5.00; the person who brought back the most pumpkins won the money. Then we played another game called, "pumpkin bombing." With this game, you needed a convertible car. Butch filled that need with a 1950 Ford convertible he owned. One night I was the bombardier, standing up in the front seat with someone in the back seat steadying me. We timed a light at an intersection so we could go through it doing about 45 miles per hour. The target was another rival corner gang. Everything was going as planned and I let loose with a bowling ball size pumpkin, hitting the wall and splattering the guys hanging out with pieces of pumpkin-a direct hit. All was good until my knee hit the door handle during this maneuver, causing the door to open and me to fall out. Fortunately, when I landed, it was on my butt with my feet out in front of me going in the same direction as the car. I can still very vividly remember sliding along with the car and remember watching as the rear wheels slowly passed by me. It was probably another fifty feet or so when I came to a stop. Luckily for me, it was a very cold night out and I had on a leather jacket and long johns under my blue jeans. The surface of the road was smooth, since it was recently repaved. These factors certainly helped my situation in that I was not killed outright. I had several months to ponder my stupidity before the scabs on my butt and elbows stopped cracking, finally allowing me to heal completely.

CHAPTER 7
JOINING THE MARINE CORPS

By the mid-nineteen-sixties, life on the old corner seemed to be changing rapidly. A lot of the group was spending more and more time away with their girlfriends. Two of the older guys, Joe and Big John, joined the Marines within six months of each other in 1964. Some of the guys were talking about joining some of the other services. Life for me at home and in school seemed to be getting worse by the day. Something had to change. I followed that old proverbial saying; "I jumped out of the frying pan into the fire." On my 18th birthday in 1965 I joined the United States Marine Corps.

My cousin Mike was supposed to join up with me on the buddy system but he backed out at the last minute, only to be drafted into the M.C. a year later. He ended up in Vietnam before I did, which I thought was quite ironic. One of the reasons I picked the Marines was my belief that they were the best fighting force in the United States, if not the world, and I wanted and liked to fight. From very early in my childhood, it became apparent to me that I had a penchant for fighting, which shouldn't be surprising because growing up in my household, meant that you often needed to fight for what you wanted. After years of putting up with the crap that my older brother Jack laid upon me, I decided to do something about it. At the age of eleven I joined the PAL [Police Athletic League] to learn how to box. The training I received over several years allowed me to become a skilled boxer and more than once that knowledge got me in and out of a lot of trouble. A good example of this was on my first day in high school at Cardinal Dougherty when we were all in assembly. There was this big black kid sitting behind me, whacking the back of my head. After he did it the third time, I stood up, turned around towards him and told him in a voice that all nearby could hear, "I'll beat the shit out of you right now if you do that again." Of course now, I knew that I was going to have to fight this guy and once we were back in our homeroom, we went at it. The fight was a short one, with my knocking him down and out. He wasn't out for long and as I was walking away he got up and came at me with a knife and was about to put it in my back. The only reason he didn't get me was because another black man, whom I met before assembly and befriended, hit him square across his chest with a wooden chair. This time he stayed down. I had met my savior in, of all places, the bathroom. He and some of his friends were "Doo-Wopping" to some songs I was familiar with and I asked if I could join them. With a surprised look on his face, followed by a large grin that exposed two gold teeth, Sonny said, "By all means, my man." I sang several songs with them until it was time to head to assembly. Later on I became friends with Tommy, the guy I knocked out and I taught him how to box. The bonus part of all this was that I got a reputation as someone you didn't want to mess with. In that school, the largest Catholic high school in the United States in 1961, this was a good thing to have, considering that the school's initials, "C.D." were also referred to stand for "CITY DUMP."

Many freshmen of Cardinal Dougherty High School in 1961 were the first to go fight in Vietnam when President Johnson called for the big buildup of troops in 1965. For our school, the results of that war produced one of the largest ratios of dead and wounded when compared to all the other high schools in the United States. It very well may have been the highest: you could fill out a full battalion with them, with over 1400 dead alone. Many of these students I knew as friends.

I didn't graduate from Cardinal Dougherty; I was thrown out in my junior year for poor grades and bad behavior. This was probably the best thing that could have happened to me. The only other high school I could go to was Cheltenham High School, which was far superior in all aspects of providing an education. My problem was the fact I just didn't fit in with most of the student population, which was composed mostly of very rich kids of the Jewish faith. One of those kids was named Netanyahu and went on to become the Prime Minister of Israel. One other famous alumnus of that school is Reggie Jackson.

The education I was receiving was a far cry from what I had experienced in the past and for the first time I was actually beginning to enjoy learning; just being in a classroom of 25 students, compared to the average of 170 students in each classroom at Cardinal Dougherty, made all the difference. However, I still got into fights and was close to getting thrown out of that school. I made the decision that it was time to see what else was out there in the world.

CHAPTER 8
BOOT CAMP

A week after my 18th birthday I was sworn into the M.C. About a month after that I reported to the Marine recruit station in Philadelphia to start my journey to Parris Island, South Carolina, to begin 13 weeks of hell in boot camp.

My last month as a civilian was a mix of joy and ecstasy, coupled with anxiety and a bit of fear. My cousin Mike and I were dating two sisters; Mike was dating Josephine and I dated her older sister, Jeri. During that month Josephine and I were drawing closer and closer towards each other. The night before I was to report for duty, the girls threw a going away party for me. Throughout the night Angel [a nickname that I liked to call Josephine] and I were trying to find reasons to get together and be close with each other. It was during one of these encounters that one of the guests caught Angel and me in a passionate kiss and yelled out his discovery. My cousin became quite angry and yelled some nasty epithets at Angel. With Jeri crying hysterically, Mike screaming at Angel, the party quickly came to an end. Angel and I dated or I should say mostly corresponded with each other for nearly the next two years and I thank her for that.

The trip from Philadelphia to Parris Island, South Carolina was first by airplane, then by bus for the final leg. I remember it well, getting off that airplane, with the warm humid southern air hitting me in the face. I remember that I liked how it felt. I got to know some of the other guys on our bus trip to the base- we were all on the same flight down from Philadelphia, but didn't connect till we got on the bus. We were all assigned to recruit platoon 123, part of the first Battalion, the "Blood and Guts Battalion". It helped my morale a lot to have these guys as friends starting boot camp. We got to know each other on the bus because of Bill Muldowney. He seemed to be an easygoing guy who could get you talking. My gut feeling about this guy was negative, telling me to not trust him, but at the same time, I was grateful that he was the one who broke the ice amongst the rest of us on the bus. Bill and I did one thing together that still may stand as a record. In a regimental contest, one of the challenges is a time trial of putting together shelter-halves to create a pup tent. We set a record, doing it in 46 seconds flat.

Boot camp was a life-changing experience for anyone who was able to get through it. When I first got there, I weighed 128 pounds and could do about 30 pushups; by the time I graduated 13 weeks later, I was 155 pounds and could do 123 pushups. My attitude also went through a major change. When I first got there it would be fair to say that the description of me as a know-it-all, teenage punk with a chip on his shoulder fit like a glove. "DI's" [Drill Instructors] had fun with guys like me. They just loved to break us down in just about every conceivable manner that they could come up with. Being able to do 123 pushups was a direct result of their psychological warfare on me. One of the DI's, more so than the others, really had it in for me. He was a tall, lanky, good-old southern boy who hated northern boys who had an attitude. The first time he physically let into me was at the rifle range. While on a forced march going to the rifle range, I did something to piss him off and he told me to report to him when we got to the barracks at the range. I hoped that he had forgotten telling me that and I didn't report to him. Later that night he called me up to the front of the barracks. He told me to stand at attention, which I was anyway, and then he hit me in the stomach as hard as he could. On the third blow, I crumbled to the ground in agony. Then in a voice it seemed only drill instructors could muster, he told me "Don't you ever disobey my orders! You got that, maggot?" I moaned, "Yes Sir." More trouble came my way the next day when I got into a fight with another recruit. Both of us were on mess duty and were in charge of two separate sculleries. I was short a man in mine and I went over to his scullery to see if he had someone to send to mine. He did, but wasn't about to give me one. We started arguing over this and it soon escalated into a shoving match that turned into a fight. I got my extra man and thought that was the end of it. About an hour later, I was told to report to the head drill instructor at our barracks. He had learned about the fight and basically told me that that was unacceptable behavior and for punishment, I was told to report to the CCP [Corrective Custody Platoon]. When I got there, another recruit and me, who was also small in stature, were given 10-pound sledge hammers, no gloves, and were told that if we didn't turn a three foot square, reinforced piece of concrete into dust in two hours, we would be spending the next two days there. All around us were recruits who were doing totally inane work, such as filling up two buckets with sand, walking a hundred yards, dump it into a pile, fill the buckets again, go back to the other pile, dump it, etc. With very bloody hands, we turned the concrete into dust with only minutes to spare.

CHAPTER 9
RIFLE RANGE

Once I had my M-14 rifle zeroed in and started to practice on the firing range, the DI's changed their attitude towards me, but not at first; you see I was doing real well on the course, but I was doing it left handed, a no-no because of some regulation. For some reason, possibly because I use my left eye when I aim in on something, is why I do it left handed, things like the game of pool, or shooting a bow-an-arrow or slingshot and in this case, my M-14 rifle. I'm ambidextrous, with my strength being in my right arm. This came in handy when boxing, more that once, with just my right jab from a southpaw stance, I knocked-out more than one opponent. I was able to convince them that it really didn't matter, after I demonstrated that I could do as fast what any right-handed shooter could do with the M-14 rifle, the DI's let me continue firing left handed.

I grew-up around weapons; my father had several old single shot 22 cal. Rifles, one of them had an octagon barrel. Our father let us use the basement for target practice. I once shot a crow right out of the air with the octagon rifle. They soon had me giving instruction to other recruits who were not doing very well. I was able to get all of them to shoot at least marksman on qualification day. As for myself, on pre-qualification day, I tied the M.C. record. On qualification day, I had a better score than the day before, going into the 500-yard line. At the 500 lines, I had adjusted my elevation sight at its near max. My first three rounds were just a bit low off dead center. It was either trying to put one more click on my elevation or try using Kentucky wind-age to center my rounds on target. The rear sight popped right out of its housing. Resetting the sight was going to change what I had zeroed my weapon on prior to the beginning of qualification. No new record was created, but I still managed to shoot a very high expert score. Each year every Marine in the M.C. had to re-qualify with the M-14 and later years the M-16 rifle, also the 45 cal. pistol. All four years that I was in the M.C. I fired high expert with all those weapons. Shooting as well as I did was probably the redeeming factor that kept the DI's from sending me back to start all over again with a new platoon.

    I'm sure the DI's were aware of my expanded group of buddies and that we pulled a "Blanket Party" on the guy that reported me to the DI's, who I learned later on was the same recruit I had the fight with. In a true blanket party, the victim would have a blanket covering him from his head to his toes and the people doing this would pin him down with the blanket. From that point on a lot of hurt could come upon the victim, it depended on what he did to have this pulled on him. We didn't hurt him any, just wanted to scare him badly. I actually became somewhat friendly with the guy before we graduated. I might add that I was in another fight while at the rifle range, one that I think the DI's instigated. The reason I think that was because they wanted me to do the same thing to another recruit they were having problems with. This recruit was one of my buddies and I made only a half-hearted attempt to get him in a fight. Another time, I was at the sink shaving. Behind me was this good old boy from Mississippi who was at least six foot two and weighed at least two hundred and twenty pounds. He was the leader of one of the other squads in our platoon and up till then I never had contact with him. When I bent down to get a drink of water he pushed me further into the sink, saying, "Your time is up," nearly breaking my teeth on the faucet in the process. Well, I turned around and put a good jab to his face. What surprised me was when he came back with his own jab, knocking me back but not down. Now I have fought guys this big before and knew I wasn't going to win a boxing match with him, so I resorted by charging him and slamming my head as hard as I could into his solar-plexus, knocking the air out of him. While doing this, I did my best to get him in a bear hug around his waist, but ended grabbing him just below his butt. For a good minute or more he pounded on my back with his fist. I finally got in a position where I was able to lift him up and at the same time flip him on his back. He came down hard on his back and head on the tiled floor, knocking him out. I never did hear anything from the DI's about this incident.

The day before we were to leave the rifle range and march back to the main base, I was in the barracks cleaning it up. One of my DI's was practicing breaking concrete slabs with his hand. This DI just got back from a judo contest; he was on the M.C. judo team. He saw me checking him out and called me over and asked me, "Think you can break one of these slabs?" "Yes sir, if I can use a rifle glove when I try sir." He said, "Sure, why not, give it your best shot." The slab was 10 X 6 X 1 inch thick, balanced on its edges between similar pieces. This would be the first time I had ever attempted to do something like this. With deep concentration and determination, I slammed the side of my closed right fist onto the slab. On my first try and to my surprise, I broke it. Feeling more confident, I asked if I could try again without the glove. The DI grumbled, "Yeah, go for it," again, success on my first try. I then asked if I could try breaking two slabs. He looked at me with part amazement and insolence and said, "If you think you can, do it." On my second try, I did it. "McNally, that was pretty impressive. I'm going to ask the captain if you can do that on graduation day." Hearing that from him was like being told I just won a million bucks. Up till then I had no idea if I was going to graduate with my platoon or not. This DI knew I was in three boxing matches or "Smokers" as the M.C. called them. These matches were held at the rifle range and he knew I won all of my fights. He then asked me, "Who do you think would win a fight between a judo expert and a boxer?" I replied, "Sir, the boxer sir, if he knew the guy he was fighting was a judo expert, sir." That not very bright comment brought our relation back into focus. In a pissed off voice, he told me to get back to cleaning up the barracks.

Back at the main base, the DI's started to treat us more like Marines. We had everyone in our platoon qualify at the rifle range. Our marching drills were nearing perfection. We were beginning to see the light at the end of the tunnel: graduation. This illusion was wiped out for me and four other recruits when we returned to the barracks after drilling on the parade grounds. The contents of our footlockers were strewn all over the squad bay floor. We committed a cardinal sin when we left our footlockers unlocked. On the floor were five combination locks, all locked together. Then the insidious game started. We were put in a circle around the locks and were told to find our individual lock, unlock it and put up our gear; sounded simple enough until we were told to start moving around in a circle while doing this. As we passed the judo expert, we got a good whack in the back with a swagger stick. On my fifth rotation, he gave me a very sharp shot and I lost it. I turned towards him with my arm cocked to punch his lights out, when the good old boy smashed me in the side of my head. His blow punctured my eardrum and I fell to the ground screaming bloody murder. What the DI's didn't know was that this had happened to me once before, on the same ear, while I was going to Cardinal Dougherty high school. Father Bennett did the same thing to me when he saw me jumping up, pulling

Christmas decorations off the ceiling. Just like the first time, the perpetrator was at a loss at what to do about his blunder. My parents considered suing the priest, but let it go when my ear healed over about a month later. In boot camp, if I went to sickbay and reported the incident, he could have been thrown out of the M.C. for such behavior. Letting him sweat it out seemed appropriate. I knew he was worried when a DI from another platoon came up to me and asked, "Are you planning on going to sickbay?" I told him, "I haven't yet decided, sir!"

The next day our platoon was out back of our barracks sitting in some bleachers and shining our dress shoes for graduation. While I was smoking a cigarette, I tried to see if I could blow smoke out of my ear, just like I did the first time this happened to me. It was easy to do: all I had to do was pinch off my nose with my fingers and try to force inhaled smoke out of my nose. The only other exit for the smoke was the ear canal so out of my ear smoke would flow. One of my other DI's was up on the second story fire escape looking down at us when he saw me doing this. This DI was the good guy out of the four and was the one who would give us encouragement and hope that someday we were going to get out of that hellhole. "McNally, get your ass up here double time." Sergeant Good Guy pulled me into the squad bay and started to tell me, "Do you have any idea how much money you can make doing what I saw you doing, well, do you?" "Yes sir, ah, no sir, I mean, I never thought about that sir." "Well, just think about how much money you could make betting someone in a bar that you can blow smoke out of your ear. Think about it, you could get rich." "Yes sir, I guess I could at that." "McNally I think you are all right. Tell you what, since you are the first Marine I ever knew who can blow smoke out of his ear, I'm going to give you a cigar and you can smoke it right here in the squad bay, how would you like that?" "Would I like to, hell sir, I'd be proud to smoke your cigar here in the squad bay." "Here's your cigar, now call the rest of the platoon up here." "As you say sir, thank you sir." "All right, now let's light up that cigar Marine." He did his job well; there was no way now I was going to report Sergeant Bad Guy to anyone.

CHAPTER 10
GRADUATION

Two days later, I graduated with Platoon 123. I now earned the title of United States Marine. That day will always be recalled as one of my fondest. My father traveled down from Philadelphia, interrupting his very busy schedule as a doctor to witness my graduation from boot camp. This meant the world to me. It was great pride I felt escorting him around the base and showing him all the obstacle courses that I had to master, remembering that it took total team-work for that to happen. Not all recruits are created equal and in the Marines the ones who were having a hard time of it got help from other recruits who were more able. Back at the barracks my father got to talk with Sergeant Judo, who described me as a good Marine with possibly great potential.

He also told my dad about my ability firing the M-14 rifle and breaking the concrete slabs [the captain wouldn't allow the demonstration.] Sergeant Bad Guy showed up while my dad and I were in the squad bay. He called me over to talk in private. I obliged him and before we were done talking we were crying and hugging each other. I'll never forget what I got out of boot camp and that was what the power of self-discipline and what teamwork can accomplish. Both have served me well ever since. I left Parris Island with the confidence that I could master anything I put mind to do. I was also beginning to appreciate what

"Semper Fidelis" [Always Faithful] meant.

The day after graduation, the platoon assembled outside the front of our barracks to find out what our individual MOS [Military Occupational Specialty]. This was a number that indicated what your job was going to be in the M.C; for the majority of us including me, that number was 0300 or infantry. That was what I was hoping to be in, or I should say, expected to be in. We were told that we have an hour to grab ass or whatever before transportation showed up to take all of us to our next duty station, Camp Geiger.

CHAPTER 11
CAMP GEIGER

Regardless of the MOS you had, you still had to go to school to be taught the skills of a basic infantryman. Camp Geiger was located in North Carolina in the same vicinity of the large base of Camp Lejeune. The time you spent there varied on what year you went through it. In my case it was seven weeks. During this time we were trained and familiarized with every conceivable weapon in the M. C. arsenal.

Several incidents stick in my mind from that period. One of them concerned a black guy, Melvin B. [who didn't want to be addressed by his first name, so I called him Mr. M] who became a friend of mine. I'm talking about a guy that I became such good friends with that we talked about opening a restaurant in Philadelphia together as partners, once we got out of the M.C. One day after we came back from the field, he had an epileptic seizure. This was the first time in my life that I saw someone have a seizure. In his case, the first seizure he had. I was at a total loss at what to do. As it turned out, it took six good size Marines to keep him from hurting himself or someone else. Three days later, he was back on full duty with us again as if nothing happened.

Then there was the time when my buddy Bill and I were on guard duty at a mess hall out in the boonies. We were told that a specialized M.C. recon unit liked to break into the mess hall to steal food. Our job was to make sure that didn't happen. This mess hall had a 40-50 yard clearing all around it. Bill and I figured we were going to have a hard time covering all that area without some kind of an early warning system in place to give us the heads up on the situation. While rummaging through a dumpster in the back of the mess hall, we were lucky enough to find several hundred yards of field communication wire and a lot of empty tin cans. With this material, we went about setting up a sound making system to give us an early warning if something was out of the ordinary. About three in the morning, our devices warned us of a breach of our lines. We stealthily maneuvered into a counter position when we saw a lone figure making his way to the mess hall. As he entered into our trap, we locked and loaded our M-14s and at the same time yelled out, "Who goes there?" A much shaken second lieutenant explained, "I'm the officer of the day, what the hell do you think you're doing?" "Just our jobs sir," we replied at the same time. He grumbled something else that was incoherent to us, turned and left. Both Bill and I laughed over that night many times.

One more person I should mention is Chief Maybee, an American Indian, who was born and raised on a reservation in upstate New York. He was one of the most complex persons that I had ever met up till that time. Not only did he graduate Private First Class from the same platoon I was in, the rank given to the top recruit in each platoon, he was promoted to Lance Corporal while still in basic infantry training. This was something that is almost unheard of in the Marine Corps. Two different occasions while I was enjoying on-base liberty, while visiting the "Slop-Sauté" [slang for the enlisted men's club] a bar that sold beer that contained minuscule amounts of alcohol, I got to see two completely opposite sides of the chief. One was the sober person who could play any song on his guitar on his first try. The other person was a guy who managed to get drunk on the beers and beat the crap out of six good size Marines. Strangely, he went AWOL [Absent With Out Leave] shortly after he got to his next duty station. The FBI captured him on the outskirts of Jacksonville, Florida on a ranch working with horses. He got a half-year in the brig, about the same amount of time that he was AWOL. The M.C. didn't discharge him when he got out of the brig - I heard later that he became a sergeant in Vietnam.

One other incident is worth mentioning and that was when our company was given an eight-hour off base liberty. We were told that we were an experimental company. How we handled ourselves on this liberty would have a lot to do if it was going to happen again. Most of us went into Jacksonville, North Carolina, a rat hole near the base whose inhabitants made their living primarily from us. Most of us got drunk. About two hours before we were due back at the base we ran into a couple of Marines who were from Camp Lejeune who saw some easy money to be made from our group of "BOOTS" or new guys. They were telling us that they would drive us back to the base before our liberty was up. They also mention that they knew a couple of black girls that just loved to get it on with Marines, if we were interested. I guess the fact that we possessed clouded, drunk minds made it sound good to my buddy Bill and me. While driving back to the base, we were all chalking it up as a good night on the town, that is, until the asshole driving told us it was going to cost $5.00 more, from each of us, for them to drive on base and deliver us to our barracks. I nearly lost it with these scumbags, but the other guys I was with convinced me to forget it; we just didn't have the time. Guess you could say that was my first lesson in anger management.

CHAPTER 12
CAMP LEJEUNE

Upon graduation, we were given our orders for our next duty station and our first real off the base thirty-day leave. Back home after all the congratulations and advice and the promises of prayers that were going to be said for me from friends and family, I found myself spending more and more time with Angel, after awhile it seemed we spent every conceivable moment we could find to be with each other. It seemed that love was in the air. After my leave was up, I reported to my first duty station, Camp Lejeune, located in North Carolina. This was the base of the Second Marine Division. My assignment was with A Company, 1st Battalion, of the 8th Regiment. A lot of my friends also got assigned to the same battalion. Chief Maybee was in the same company as me, that's why I knew what happened to him. Bill was with B Company, which was sent to Panama for six months of jungle training shortly after he got there. The unit I joined had been involved in the Santa Domingo crises and had just returned from there. For the next six months all we did was train, train and train some more in infantry tactics. During the rare times we were back at the barracks and not out in the field training, we played cards or went into Jacksonville to party. On the very rare times when I could get a three or four day pass, I would, anyway I could, go home to see Angel. One of those times I almost didn't complete my journey. On one trip up to Philadelphia, with the car loaded with other Marines, I had a blowout of the right rear tire of old reliable, a 1964 Ford Falcon station wagon that was handed on down through our family. This happened, fortunately for us, when we came to a near standstill in traffic that had slowed down due to an accident. Just prior to this, I was doing about seventy miles per hour. It made me think, was it just pure sheer chance or was my Guardian Angel working on my behalf again?

CHAPTER 13
MED-CRUISE

After about a half year at Camp Lejeune, our battalion shipped off for a six-month tour in the Mediterranean and surrounding seas and oceans. All of us referred to this as the Med-Cruise, which was a coveted tour of duty. Our company was on the Sandoval [APA 194], which was a flat bottom troop carrier. On the bulkhead, by the stairwell going from the main deck up to the bridge of the ship, was a plaque that described and saluted the fact that the ship and most of its men had survived three separate kamikaze attacks that occurred during World War II in the Pacific Ocean. To say the least, living conditions aboard ship were horrendous. Forget air-conditioning, it didn't exist; it hovered around 90 degrees in our compartment throughout the trip. We were packed in like sardines in a can, rows of five racks that went straight up. The top four were for sleeping, the bottom one to stow our sea bags. Lying on your back, your face was about eight inches from the rack above you. It got particularly bad when we were in port for liberty; Marines would come back to the ship drunk and many times they would vomit the night's load out the side of their rack. Pity the poor fools who were beneath them.

As our fleet sailed to the Mediterranean Sea, I was on guard duty in one of the cargo holds guarding a few jeeps and piles of sleeping mattresses that were all about. My mistake was falling asleep on one of them. I got caught and for punishment, I was restricted to the ship for our first liberty, lost two weeks of pay and had to spend time in the bilge of the ship, scraping rust off the bulk heads. While in the bilge on my second day, a steam pressure valve released on my back when I was under it. If it weren't for the fast action of the Navy guy who worked there, I could have ended up with worse burns than what I got. He heard my scream and immediately pulled me out from under the decking and covered my back with bilge grease. By doing this, he prevented blistering from forming on the second-degree burns that I received.

The rest of my time in the bilge was cancelled. Being restricted to the ship during our first liberty worked out to my advantage. With only half of my pay, I got into a blackjack game the night before we pulled into Rota, Spain. Early on in the game, I had won several times and then got a blackjack. If you won with a blackjack, you had the option of taking the deal. I counted my money and figured I could cover the cost if I were to lose to everyone on the first deal, so I took it. It was to be my night; I walked away with $475.00. During the time we were in port, I lent it all out, with interest. By the end of that cruise, I had loan sharked enough to collect over $2000.00. When word got around that I was in this business, I got a visit from the two other loan sharks amongst the Marines, Venatolia and Sanuchi, two very bad dudes from New York City. They just wanted to make sure I wasn't lending out money to any of their clients. As long as I didn't, they told me, all I had to do was mention their names if someone didn't want to pay up and if that didn't work; they would collect the money for me; never had to do that.

As you may imagine, I had a great time in the other 22 liberty ports we visited. Naples, Italy was the first port I got to enjoy liberty in, acquiring a nice push-button knife and a thin bladed banana knife to carry in my combat boot. I bought these knives from a character that scared the hell out of me when he first came out of the shadows in a deserted alleyway. He was a very large man who was wearing a full-length black trench coat, which he opened up to reveal a very large assortment of knives, saying at the same time, "Hey Marine, want to buy a knife?" Six days later, we arrived at Lama De Revelino, Italy for a landing exercise. Our ship then spent a little over a week in Trieste, Italy. This was the first time in 30 years that a U.S. ship was allowed back in that port; 30 years past, it seemed some kind of riot occurred, where some of the local population ended up dead, hence we were not allowed back there until now. When it came to the prostitutes of that port, it was like going back in some kind of a time warp. I'm sure some of the ladies plied their trade the last time a Navy ship was in that port. I'm not complaining, mind you, because my memories of that port are rather fond. It was off to Corfu, Greece for another week of liberty. Don't remember much about this port. Must have drunk some of the local Ouzo, a drink we were warned not to drink, it was told to us it could cause blindness. I had the bad habit of doing what I was told not to do back then, guess I wanted to find out first hand why we were told not to do something. I didn't go blind but I did know someone who was close to it for over three days.

In Lebedos Bay, Turkey the fleet was involved in a weeklong exercise with NATO troops. I remember the terrain here was particularly rugged. One Marine broke his back when he slipped off a cliff edge. Scorpions that were everywhere stung other Marines. I think it was in this country, while another Marine and I were on an outpost assignment, decided to sneak on down to this country village that was directly beneath our location. We figured we could trade some cigarettes for a bottle of wine and maybe some fresh bread and have ourselves a good night while we occupied our position. Well, for once, we actually got away with doing something like this. They were very nice people down in that village, and seemed to be very appreciative that we were here training with their troops and gave us a good deal on the wine and bread.

The most embarrassing event happened when someone was found infested with crabs. As a prevention of infesting the ships with them, we all had to strip down, get inspected and then dusted before we could return to the ships. On a sad note, we were told about a young Shepherd boy getting killed when he wandered into a live firing range. He detonated an unexploded mortar round. From Turkey, it was back to Naples for two more weeks of fun, then a bit more than a week in Golfe Juan, France. More exercises were held on Sardinia. From there it was back to Italy with nearly two weeks of liberty in Livorno. The fleet then went to Timbakion, Crete for a week in the field training. Of all the liberty ports, the last ones in Spain were my favorite, a week in Valencia and two more in Barcelona. Both of the ports were very clean and attractive in overall architecture and design. Prostitution seemed much more accepted as well, the women I met were far more liberated, better dressed and as a whole, better off than the ones I met prior on this cruise. On the other hand, both of the ports also had the dubious title of the ports with the highest level of venereal diseases amongst its prostitutes, throughout the Mediterranean Sea area. I guess I was lucky that I didn't come down with one of these dreadful diseases. The first night I was in Valencia, I met this very attractive lady who promised to explore with me all of the sexual positions she knew, so I could brag to my buddies of her sexual prowess. It was quite a night and several other nights with her as well.

Barcelona was much different. I had gone into what I thought was an upscale restaurant and bar to eat and drink. While sitting at the bar, a very attractive lady sat down next to me. She had a striking resemblance to Angel; she may have been a few years older than Angel and a bit curvier, but presented a much more mature, worldly woman who was in total control of her life. The girl I left at home was just beginning to find and develop such a nature. In nearly flawless English, with just a bit of a Spanish accent, she started up a conversation with me. I was taken aback at first; I couldn't believe this goddess was talking to me. I was even more surprised when she offered me her hand while introducing herself to me. The texture of her skin was smooth as a baby's ass and it wasn't only her hands that felt that way, I was to find out that every inch of her body felt the same. At first, I thought she might be some kind of spy, from the kind of questions she was asking me. Later, as the conversation went on, I realized that she was looking for a particular type, a person who would spend his entire liberty exclusively with her. She was not like any of the other prostitutes I've met; for one thing, it wasn't wham, bam, and thank you madam. We spent the days and nights of my liberty together exploring Barcelona, savoring every last minute of it. I didn't want it to end and found it difficult to leave when it was time to depart. Two days later we anchored off Almeria, Spain and turned over command to Battalion 2/6 and departed for the United States.

CHAPTER 14
BACK TO CAMP LEJEUNE – FOR NEW ORDERS

On our trip back, we ran into one of the first hurricanes of the season. For three days we were in its grip. I'm pretty sure that all on board got sea sick during this time; on the third day the Captain of the ship got on the intercom and admitted to being sick too, but urged us to hang in there and do the best we could do under the circumstances. It was a very, very rough three days.

Once we were back in the good old USA, during the first week back at Camp Lejeune, I got a 30 day leave and my orders for my next duty station, Camp Pendleton, California; where for three months, I went through so called jungle training to prepare me to be able to fight in Vietnam. Other than getting into great shape while we traversed the lovely mountains that were on the base, I don't think a whole lot of what we were taught really prepared you for what Vietnam had in store for each individual. I will admit that I did learn some things about the booby traps that I was soon to encounter.

I spent my 30-day leave back home and like the first time home on leave, I devoted most of my time to be with Angel. Knowing now that I would be going to Vietnam, our relationship took on new meaning and by the end of my leave; Angel and I were beginning to think about getting married. I even gave her an engagement ring that I won in a card game.

I was never completely comfortable with Angel, in that I found it way too easy getting close with her when my cousin Mike was dating her. If I could do it, what was to stop her the next time she sees someone else she takes a liking to? My cousin Mike was and still is a bit of a "Dapper-Dan," a type guy a lady wouldn't want to lose. Why she wanted me over him, I was never too sure. I just had a gut feeling about it all, but I had a lot of confidence in that feeling.

All too quickly, my leave came to an end and before I knew it, I was at the Philadelphia airport getting ready to fly out to Camp Pendleton, California. This would be the second departure out of this airport where friends and family were present to see me off to some location in the Marine Corps. Unlike the first time, when there was plenty of fun and gaiety, this time was much more sobering, knowing it would be the last time any of them would see me before I went to Vietnam. The last ten minutes or so became very emotional; all of them were acting as though I wasn't coming back. I am not too sure why they were coming off like that because I never had any doubt about that outcome.

CHAPTER 15
CRUISE SHIP TO VIETNAM

Three months later, after completing training at Camp Pendleton, on October 3rd, 1966, I left San Diego, California for a twenty-two day trip to Vietnam. The ship that I traveled to Vietnam on, called the USNS Barrett, was once a cruise ship, converted into a troop carrier, whose living conditions were a far cry better than the ship I did the Med-cruise on. For one thing, we had individual beds to sleep on, not the stacked up racks we had on the Med-Cruise and air conditioning, something I wouldn't get to experience again until six months later when I went on R&R [Rest and Recuperation] to Kowloon, part of mainland China. Aboard the ship were a fairly large Army artillery unit and about a hundred individual Marines who were going to different locations in Vietnam. It was a pretty relaxed trip, with none of the normal duties to perform like we had to carry out while on the Med-Cruise. I got to fight in another boxing smoker. I didn't mention it before, but while I was on the Med- Cruise I got to fight in six smokers. In the first one, I fought another guy from our team, as the ship we were fighting against didn't have someone in my weight class. For some reason and I'm not sure why, I forgot everything I was ever taught and tried to bully my way through this fight and ended up losing by decision. The next day our team was on the fantail of the ship working out. A lot of the guys were ribbing me about my losing the fight and I kept telling them that it was just a fluke. Well, the guy who I fought was hearing all of this and butted in, saying, "Boy, I can kick your ass anytime." I replied, "Well, now is anytime." We got gloves and went at it. This time it seemed everything I had ever learned in boxing came to fruition; and I put enough shots to his left eye that it caused so much bruising and swelling that the captain said he could not fight that night in the smoker; and I could. From that night on, I went on to win all my matches. I had a really talented boxing coach in my corner. He went by the name of Albert, because his Korean-Puerto Rico name was too hard to pronounce. He was from a tough neighborhood, Bedford Stuyvesant, part of Brooklyn, New York City; and won the Golden Gloves Championship before he joined the Army and became the top boxer in his weight class on the Army's boxing team. After six years of doing that, he transferred to the Marines to get on their boxing team. He was given sleeping quarters in our barracks, when one day he was horsing around with a guy who was much bigger than he was. Well, the big guy put a hard shot to Albert's chest, cracking his sternum, effectively ending his chance to get on the boxing team and consequently he was assigned to our unit until a later date. The second time when our ship was in Naples, Italy while on the Med-Cruise, I got to fight at a very fancy club in that city against an Italian boxing team. I was part of the team the fleet put together to fight this team and was one of the few who won his match. My fight was a quick one when I got lucky and knocked out my opponent in the first round in 47 seconds. It turned out that the guy I beat went on to fight with the Italian Olympic boxing team in the 1968 Olympics.

Back on board the USNS Barrett, I won my boxing match against an Army guy that turned into a pretty bloody affair; his blood was flowing from several places out of his face. During that same week on October 16, 1966, our ship, at the latitude of 29 degrees, crossed the 180th Meridian and

I was initiated into the Royal Domain of The Golden Dragon. The initiation consisted of crawling on your belly, on the deck of the ship, through a gauntlet of sailors and Marines who had already been through the initiation. The deck where you crawled was flooded with water and filled with the day's garbage from the mess hall. Throughout this whole ordeal, you were getting whacked, mostly in the butt, with the end of wet towels. At the end of the gauntlet you were introduced to "King Neptune" where you got to kiss his bilge-greased fat belly. That was one of the highlights aboard that ship while crossing the Pacific Ocean and was a good day to remember. I still have my membership card indicating that I had been initiated.

CHAPTER 16
OKINAWA

Two days out of Vietnam we made a short stop in Okinawa at a place called Red Beach. The ships passengers were given an eight-hour on-base leave. The only entertainment on the base was the enlisted men's club. By now, I realized that the only thing that could come out of putting a bunch of Army and Marines together and mix in some booze was just what happened; one hell of a mob fight. I decided early on that I didn't want any part of what I knew what was going to happen and decided to make love and not war. Hiding in the trunk of a taxi, my buddy and me got off the base to the kind of place I asked the driver to take us to. The place was not far from the base; it had just what I was looking for, some good-looking ladies of the night. The situation we found was nearly the opposite of what you would find on a Med-Cruse. In Okinawa, we were treated as if we were family. First we ate dinner with the family and then given baths and a massage before we retired to separate rooms with our ladies; saying that it was a good time would be an understatement. Our taxi returned at the designated time and he got us back on base to make the midnight curfew. Getting back on the ship took longer than I thought it would because we had to maneuver around and over bloody Army and Marine bodies that were lying and groaning all over the place. It must have been one hell of a brawl.

CHAPTER 17
ARRIVAL IN VIETNAM

A few more days at sea brought us to our destination, the port of Da Nang, Vietnam. The ship docked and we were getting ready to disembark when the odors of this country hit me. I had never smelled anything quite like it before. The smell emanated was coming from food cooking, the livestock and the exhaust of vehicles and machinery. The city and its people were also amazing; I simply had never experienced anything like this before. It was truly different from any place that I've ever been to. It was a sea of people involved in a myriad of activity, in some of the most squalid conditions I ever witnessed.

We disembarked from the ship and were driven to the Da Nang air base by military buses and taken to a very large induction building. Here we were separated first by services then, according to our individual orders, to groups and separated into even smaller groups until we were finally told where to go to get to our duty stations. The second day at the base, I and some other FNGs [Fucking New Guys] got a helicopter ride about 60 miles south to the Chu Lai air base. From that base, I got a truck ride 15 miles north up Highway 1 to Hill 54, the main base of the First Battalion, Fifth Regiment, First Marine Division. I didn't know it at the time, but I just had been assigned to the most decorated Regiment that ever fought in all of the Marine Corps history. One of its nicknames was the "FIGHTING

FIFTH." At this base, I was assigned to the third squad, second platoon, of Delta Company. Sergeant Holler was my squad leader and Lance Corporal McKinley, my fire team leader. On the morning of my third day in Vietnam, I went to the battalion armory to finally get issued web gear and an M-14 rifle. I felt very naked and unnerved being in this country without this equipment.

The next day started out like all the other days since I've been in Vietnam, hot and humid, the same kind of day I would be spending in the surf off the beach of good old Wildwood, New Jersey. The thought of being there was nearly overpowering to me. It was hard for me to believe that ocean was on the other side of this planet.

Even if the hot humid conditions were bad, it was far more bearable than the annual monsoon season, when it rains so heavy and for so long you truly wondered if you were ever going to see the sun shine again. When I first came to this country, the annual monsoon was nearing its end. Everything was a sea of mud, no matter what you were doing; the mud seemed to find its way everywhere. I had been in Vietnam a little over a week and up to now all I was doing was just getting used to the climate while filling sand bags, or other such monotonous work. I did get a break from the routine drudgery when our squad was sent on a convoy as part of the security detail. One thing that stuck in my mind about this otherwise uneventful trip to the city of Quang Ngai, located about twenty miles south of the Chu Lai air base, off Highway 1, was when our trucks started picking up speed as we approached this village. I thought this was probably a security measure, but when the men in all the trucks started throwing unopened C-ration cans in a menacing way at the children converging on the convoy, I thought it strange and asked my squad leader what the hell was going on. He smirked, when telling me, "You'll be doing the same thing soon enough." A week later, I heard about another convoy going through that same village, where a child got close enough to lob a hand grenade into one of the trucks, killing three Marines and wounding four others. My first lesson on how life was going to be like in this war was sinking into my brain.

The first true combat operation that I got to participate in happened about three weeks after I got in country. Delta Company was to go into "Happy Valley," on a search and destroy mission to destroy a Viet Cong unit that was coming out of there to ambush and set up booby traps against the Marines that were out on patrol securing the Chu Lai air base. Happy Valley was a generic name the Marines gave to a series of valleys formed in a mountain chain that ran parallel two to three miles inland from the coast of the South China Sea. A happy place it wasn't, mostly jungle, narrow footpaths, terrain where the enemy could be only a few feet from you, or where you could step on a plunger or trip a wire that could set off one of their insidious booby traps.

This operation started that night in what I thought was complete insanity. Beginning in the early afternoon, monsoon rains returned; about midnight, our company moved out from our base, Hill 54. Our base was about a mile east of the mountain chain and the coast about the same distance further east. When the company moved out off Hill 54, it was unbelievably black outside with the monsoon rain coming down in buckets. Since you couldn't see your own hand in front of your face, we had to grab hold of the pack on the back of the Marine in front of us for guidance. It was tricky going down the hill into the rice paddies, which were so completely flooded, that when you were walking on top of a rice paddy dike you were in about a foot and a half of water. If you slipped off a dike, you were in water above your waist, in my case up to my chest. That was my situation when we came to a halt. Someone got lucky and broke a leg, probably by slipping off a rice paddy dike. We stayed in position until a helicopter managed to come in during a lull in the storm and got him out, about two hours later. An hour or so after that, I finally got to the other side of the rice paddies and was very relieved to be out of that water. The company bivouacked for the rest of the night at the foot of the mountains. I was so exhausted that all I could do was to wrap up in my poncho and lie on the ground and try to sleep.

The next morning, the rain had stopped and it looked like it was going to turn into a nice day. As the company was preparing to move out, I decided to put on some dry socks. I noticed as I was unlacing my boots that my feet felt and looked like they had swollen. I realized I had developed a severe case of immersion foot, just like what your hands and feet look like after being in a hot tub of water too long; my feet were all shriveled up, soft and wrinkly, like the skin on a prune. In my case, it was so bad that just the act of removing my socks was enough to break the skin on my feet. This was to be a lucky break for me and the other fourteen Marines, who were also new to this country and whose feet, like mine, were not up to all that water. By the time I left this country, the soles on my feet would turn from being soft to quarter-inch thick pieces of callus skin. The company commander decided to leave us behind to provide extra security for the radio relay team that was setting up on top of the same mountain we slept at the bottom of the night before.

The next two weeks gave me time to appreciate just how beautiful to the eye Vietnam is. The weather was perfect. The monsoon rains we encountered were to be the last I would have to endure in Vietnam. I almost felt like I was on vacation.

We dug our foxholes and set up sound making devices and a demolition expert went about setting up a pattern that could set off two hand grenades at a time when tripped or, at his discretion, set off whole sections of the rigged hand grenades that he had set all around us on the mountain, nearly to the bottom on the Happy Valley side. With all of this in place, we settled in for a pleasant two weeks. Most of this time, all we were doing was taking it easy, lying out in the sun, soaking up its pleasant rays, or we would go down to the spring-fed pool half way down the mountain on the rice paddy side and enjoy a nice dip in it. We did have some adrenalin pumping moments when a few of the hand grenades went off, mostly during the nights. I believe animals set them off; being there wasn't any follow-up action after they went off. One morning, we spotted a deer down at the base of the mountain on the Happy Valley side. Two Marines went down to hunt it without any luck. The next morning we spotted it again. This time the deer didn't luck out. In the supplies that we received by helicopter were several cases of hand grenades and M72 LAAWs, the latter a type of RPG [Rocket Propelled Grenade] that were used to take out tanks or fortified bunkers. Three Marines aimed in with the M72s and fired at the same time. There wasn't enough of that deer left to even consider trying to eat any of it.

From the many radio reports we received from our company, there was one about my squad setting off a booby trap that wounded three Marines. I couldn't help but wonder if I had been with them when it went off, would I have been wounded or killed? We finally got the orders to pack it all up and get ready to head on back to the base. There was just one problem - we still had all the hand grenades to dismantle and not enough time to do it. Sure enough, when our demolition expert pulled on all the cords at the same time, the whole mountain all around us went off in one hell of an explosion that was witnessed from our base, I heard later that he had some explaining to do to his superiors after we got back to the base. My life back on Hill 54 settled into a pretty regular routine you would expect a PFC [Private First Class] to find in a combat zone with the M.C. - lots of tedious jobs that could never be done enough to please your superiors.

I was getting to know the guys in my platoon and they were getting to know me, and I was hoping to fit in with them. We had quite a collection of characters. Most of these guys were part of the original group of Marines that secured the Chu Lai area from the sea. The landing itself was unopposed, the only thing that got in their way were the reporters of the TV networks NBC, CBS, and ABC, who filmed the landing from the beaches of Chu Lai. This was the first war where you got to digest the realities of war along with your dinner while you watched your favorite nightly TV news station. The landing was on all the news stations the next night in the USA. Actually, the enemy would have had no possible chance to hinder the landing itself, for the terrain was flat and sandy for miles in all directions. From the time this beach and the area around it were secured and the air base established, it had not been attacked, not while the Marines were securing it. The 7th and 5th Marine Regiments were set up as satellite bases around the air base and patrolled a 30-mile radius from the center of the air base. Not much went on in this area that we were not aware of or in control of. This didn't happen overnight and it took several battalion size operations and a lot of spilled blood to get this area secured that way.

CHAPTER 18
LIBERTY LIVES

War stories were common conversation among the men of our platoon, but the ones about one of the men were hard to believe, even when you knew them to be true. John Liberty was his name; his friends called him "Big John". As his nickname implies, he was a rather large man to find in the infantry. He was from New York City and was very streetwise. One of the stories was about the time his platoon was crossing a rice paddy when it came under fire. Without giving it a second thought, he charged a machine gun some fifty yards to his front. There was no cover for him to use while doing this. As he got closer, a hand grenade was thrown at him. He caught the grenade in the air and threw it back at them, killing the two V.C. [Viet Cong], who were firing the machine gun at him. Big John lived a life in Vietnam unlike any other Marine I ever heard of or knew. His actions in the field were unmatched in cunning abilities and bravery. Back out of the field and combat, the stories were just as notorious. One of those stories was about anytime his unit returned to base; John would head for the village just outside the gates of our base, not to be seen again, until it was time to return to the field. What he did there is anybody's guess, because John was a very private person and never talked about his personal life. For some unknown reason, John had a complete disrespect for most officers. I heard he even told a general to get fucked once when he was trying to present a Bronze Star to John. Let's just say that there was a love-hate situation between the brass and him. When I first met Big John, his tour was half over and his superiors wanted him to extend it. The brass had him over a barrel, he had committed offenses that got him 54 Office Hours which would be the same as a civilian getting charged with a crime and having to go to court 54 times. The choice that they gave him was that if he completed only his present tour they would give him an Undesirable Discharge at the end of it, but if he extended his tour for six more months they would guarantee him an Honorable Discharge and would drop any charges against him as long as he cooperated with them. John took them up on their offer because he knew by extending his tour for six months or more, he would automatically get to go on a free 30-day leave back to the U.S. or any other reasonable place of his choice. When the time came to where he could take this leave, I'm willing to bet that in our battalion more money was either lost or won than any other thing that may have been wagered on during that conflict; in this case, whether Big John was going to come back or not. He never did come back and not long after he was supposed to, rumors started going around that he drove a car into a stone wall at 90 miles per hour, killing him. If I knew Big John like I thought I did, that wasn't him in that car. Liberty lives.

If Big John did die in that car crash, he must have had one hell of a good time before he did because he went on leave with over $3,000 and had that much more owed to him. John had incredible luck, not only in the field but also in poker. I remember one game that both John and I were in where he had us nearly wiped out and where he was nearly wiped out himself on some Vietnamese rotgut, or their version of whiskey. Bad stuff to say the least, because the next thing we knew John just jumped up threw over the card table and ran out of the tent we were playing in. We went outside looking for him and found him by his moans. He really must have been nuts because he dove into concertina wire. That's barbed wire that lies in a coil, kind of like a big slinky toy. He must have had at least 200 puncture wounds in him, some near his eyes. Lucky for him, though, none of them caused any severe damage; never did find out why he did that fool thing. I guess the war mixed with rot-gut can cause some people to do some crazy things.

CHAPTER 19
RUNNING POINT

There is one other thing I would like to mention about Big John and that's about a position most Marines will avoid if possible and that is running point. This is the position the lead man is in for any movement in a combat situation, kind of like the Indian scout who worked for the Army Cavalry back in the 1800's when this country was trying to conquer the western frontier. The similarity of the jobs were the same, except in Vietnam, the enemy was very good at setting up booby traps that could kill or maim you, along with being able to pull off effective ambushes. Well, this was the position Big John took anytime we went to the field. He was a natural at this position; it was like he had a sixth sense. He never had any problems recognizing signs indicating enemy presence was in the area or any signs left to warn any of their own unsuspecting troops of possible booby traps or ambushes. Near the end of my time spent behind him in the bush, he seemed to literally feel if anything was wrong or out of place. Big John was my teacher. My first couple of months or so in Vietnam was spent right behind him anytime we went to the field and he was in the point position. Every time he saw something indicating the enemy had been in the area, he would show me. If he felt anything was wrong or out of place, he told or showed me about it. It wasn't very long before I became a fair point man myself.

CHAPTER 20
TET - 1967

Just before the 1967 Tet [New Year] holiday our platoon was sent to a mountain just south of the Chu Lai air base to take over part of the positions the 7th Marine Regiment normally held - who were out on an operation. This is the place Big John dove into the concertina-wire. During one night there I was on guard duty in a bunker that overlooked Hwy. 1. I was watching a single two-ton truck heading for the air base when one hell of an explosion destroyed it, blowing it into pieces. The Marine driving it was killed. About a week later, when I was reading the Philadelphia Inquirer, a newspaper that my father sent to me, it had a story in it about one of the guys from the Smigel's Corner neighborhood getting killed in Vietnam. After reading the story, I realized that it was the same person I saw killed when the truck was blown-up. I believe his name was John Iseley, who was a nice guy I knew that lived in the area. The V.C. that electronically detonated the bomb that blew-up that truck started firing on a South Korean Marine patrol that was nearby on Hwy. 1. The V.C. was firing from a nearby village. When these Marines were done, everything that was alive in that village was killed, and then the village was burned to the ground. They did this because in their mind the village people had to be V.C. sympathizers when they let this V.C. use their village.

CHAPTER 21
FIRST COMBAT

It was the second operation I went on that I was the point man. The operation was a rather large one, with South Vietnamese troops and South Korean Marines joining our battalion. Our company was on line and were combing through a lightly wooded area when we came up to a twenty-foot wide irrigation ditch and a path that ran along the ditch. We got orders to come to a halt as the other segments of our troops maneuvered into position. I was on the far right of our line and was looking down this trail when I spotted three black-clad Vietnamese running across the trail further down. The first thing that went through my mind was V. C. Both Big John and I went after them. I ran 20 to 30 yards when I caught sight of them again. On my M-14 rifle was attached a grenade launcher with a grenade ready to be fired. A cartridge made for that purpose fired it. The last time I fired a grenade was when I was going through ITR [Infantry Training Regiment] after boot camp and I think I got to do that only a few times. I'm telling this because when I aimed in on them and fired as they were crossing a bamboo footbridge, I undershot them by some 25 yards, making a big splash in the irrigation ditch but nothing else. To add to my embarrassment, I couldn't get the launcher off my weapon. The launcher fits over the flash suppressor, which in turn took away some of the recoil of the weapon when fired. With the flash suppressor covered with the launcher, it fired like an elephant gun, giving you one hell of kick to your shoulder. This probably also affected the trajectory of the round coming out of the barrel, for I aimed to kill but ended up hitting one V.C. in the foot as they were crossing the foot bridge. What I didn't see them do was practically cut this bridge in half. As I was crossing it, the bridge collapsed under me and into the water I went over my head, with pack, and rifle. Luckily, it was only deep and not wide. I got to the other side with no problem. I threw my soaked rifle up on the sandy bank and crawled up to it. When I got up on top of the bank, I could see two of the V.C. about a hundred yards away making tracks. I opened fire on them, but it was to be their lucky day because I don't think I hit either one, or at least they didn't give any indication that they were.

Not so for the one I got in the foot. This V.C. was a young girl who was about sixteen years of age. She was a very beautiful girl and at first I kind of felt bad about shooting her. I didn't feel that way for long. Upon searching her and near-by I found enough supplies and ammo for her to cause a lot of hell for us for a good month. I wondered how many people this beautiful girl was involved in killing.

As the rest of the company moved up to where I was, I continued checking her equipment. Several Marines were milling around her while a Corpsman, that's what a Medic is called in the M. C., was treating her foot. At this point I was to witness some of the brutality of war. You see, some of these Marines had been in Vietnam for some time and they had friends either killed or maimed by V.C. and what was so frustrating for them was the fact that they rarely got to see their enemy. Now they had one captured and a good-looking one to boot. They started getting very rough with her, yelling obscenities and physically abusing her. What really surprised me was when the corpsman started cutting off her blouse and undergarments. A few minuets later, I was sure she was about to get raped- but, lucky for her, the platoon sergeant came up and put a stop to it. I was surprised later when I heard that she had her foot amputated, it didn't look that bad to me for that to happen. That was hearsay talk, which wasn't the most accurate form of communication in Vietnam. For some reason, I hoped it wasn't true.

CHAPTER 22
TUNNEL RAT

The operation continued for about one more week. During this time I got my first taste of being a "Tunnel Rat". A tunnel rat was the person who went into the tunnels the V.C. dug to avoid troops, aircraft and artillery. It wasn't until long after the war that we got to realize just how extensive and elaborate their systems were; they had dug over a two hundred mile system from Cambodia to the Saigon area alone. Read the book called "The Tunnels of Cu Chi", by Tom Mangold/John Penycate to learn all about that system.

While I was traveling to Vietnam aboard the USNS Barrett, I read a story in "Reader's Digest" about tunnel rats. It was in this story that I learned of a tool used in tunnels that saved my life. Your basic tools when you went into a tunnel consisted of a flashlight, a 45 cal. pistol, a knife and earplugs. If you didn't have earplugs, filters off cigarettes crumbled and rolled up and doused with some water worked somewhat. There was one other piece of equipment to take and I would not have it if I hadn't read that story and that was a dental mirror attached to the end of a three-foot long stick. I'm a realist, because I am physically small in size, I knew I would be asked to do this job. I figured since I had experience already of going in tunnels and loved doing it, I thought I would be pretty good doing this job. While still aboard ship, I had written a letter to my parents and family and added to the contents of the supplies my father said he would send me, a dental mirror, but didn't say what I wanted it for. I learned from the story that the tunnels weren't always straight but often had 90-degree turns in them. This is where the stick with the dental mirror came in; if you came up to one of these turns you would extend the stick mirror end first to where it was in the bend of the tunnel and then you would shine your flashlight on it. You were just hoping who ever was at the other end would think that the light reflecting off the mirror was someone in the tunnel coming at them and would shoot at the light. It was in the second tunnel I went in that day in this village that I came up to one of these turns about twenty yards into it and sure enough, when I tried my little trick, I got a burst of fire from where they were, ringing my ears and shaking me up a bit. I backed up, pulled the pin on a fragmentation grenade then sent it their way. I was just getting out of the tunnel when it went off. After the smoke cleared, I went back into the tunnel and found two dead V.C.; they both had been wounded before because they had dressings on their old wounds. I guess their outfit left them behind, hoping we wouldn't find them.

There were people in the first tunnel I went into, but they were just the very old and very young members of this village. As I was handing this frightened, naked, young little girl out of the entrance of the tunnel, she pissed all over me.

The operation came to an end without any casualties to our outfit and not much more action for us than what I mention. I have to tell you, this was the most action I was to be involved in for the next five months, other than the time I nearly got killed by a water buffalo. During this period our unit was involved in a total of six operations; I participated in four of them. The operations that I didn't participate in happened when I was either on mess duty or guarding the air base, each for a month, when these other operations occurred. On the ones I participated in, there were lots of booby traps and some occasional sniper fire, but that was the extent of it. The enemy just wouldn't commit to any kind of engagement with us.

Having a water buffalo trying to kill me happened when our company was online while crossing a rice paddy when a large group of water buffalo started getting spooked by us and started breaking up in separate groups. One of the groups was making their way to the right flank of our line, when two of them started making a beeline at the last two guys in that line who just happen to be Big John and me. I had never been involved in any dealings with this kind of beast and was not at all sure what to do. When the two of them started making a charge at us, the Marine to my left fired and dropped the lead one and I was about to take out the other one, when I had the only jam I would ever have with my M-14 rifle. I believe "Oh Shit" was my first thought when this happened. I was just about to get run over when Big John took it out with his 45 cal pistol. It dropped dead, falling within a foot of me, scaring the shit out of me. Big John just gave me a wink and we moved on.

Later on, during this same operation, fate was again on my side. I was at point again when word was passed up to me to come to a halt. Our company had been following this trail along the side of a large rice-paddy when I got this order. Had this order got to me just one minute sooner it may have been me that stepped on the booby trapped mine when we were given the order to turn right and proceed on-line across the rice -paddy. A Marine who was the third man behind me was the one who stepped on the mine; his boot with his foot still in it landed next to me.

CHAPTER 23
R&R

With the arrival of April 1967, I was feeling quite refreshed. The main reason being I just got back from R&R, from Kowloon, China. Within three hours of arriving in that country, I met a prostitute that I'll never forget. Mimi Ma was her name and for five of the most exciting days of my life, she and I lived the "Good Times," while she took me throughout all that Kowloon had to offer. I was in love with her by the third day there and I think her with me. Back then, when I left her to go back to Vietnam, I was already thinking of ways I could get back to see her again. Unfortunately, this was not to be, but her letters she sent to me saved my life once I got back in Vietnam, as you'll learn later on in this story.

CHAPTER 24
MESS DUTY

The other reason I was feeling good was because I was on mess duty for the second time just before I went on R&R. Generally mess duty was not a desirable job in the Marines. Vietnam was the exception to that thought. Mess duty in Vietnam for thirty days kept you out of any duty associated with the infantry. Being a "GRUNT" meant going out on operations, patrols, ambushes, and search and destroy missions, or guard duty on one of the regimental bases or going on convoys as security. Being on mess duty gave you a much better chance of staying alive by not being shot at or setting off one of the enemy's insidious booby traps. For a month, mess duty allowed you to have some decent food everyday, as opposed to eating C-rats. When your shift was up, you had no more duties to perform until your next shift. The time off, among other things, allowed you to go to the outdoors "Movie Theater" which usually showed old war movies.

It was one night while at the movies that I smoked pot for the first time. I was sitting on a row of sandbags set up as seats to watch the movie when a couple of brothers from my platoon passed me a joint to smoke. I was smoking a cigarette when they did this and said I had a butt to smoke. They snickered when I said that and told me what they were passing was not a cigarette; it took me a few moments to realize what they were talking about. Then I thought, why not, I was on a secured base with no responsibilities other than mess duty, what could go wrong? Well, I had no idea that you were supposed to take one hit off the joint and pass it back to them. Instead, I smoked more than half of the joint before they told me to stop hogging it. What followed was probably very funny to all around watching the movie, as it was to me for most of the night. It turned out that it was not just a joint of marijuana, but one that had been dipped in opium. After about twenty minutes passed, I asked when and how is this stuff going to affect me. They just snickered again when telling me "Just give it a bit more time and you'll know." The first indication came when my shoulder started feeling weird and started getting very heavy, like someone was putting all his weight on my shoulder. Before I knew it, I fell off the sandbags and was pinned to the ground by my shoulder, hysterically laughing my ass off the whole time. After a bit of time, the weight would disperse and I would get back up on the sandbags for the next surprise. For nearly the next two hours, this phantom weight would hit my body someplace and off the sandbags I would go again, still laughing. It wasn't until after the movie was over that I lost the humor of what this drug was doing to me. I slid off the sandbags hoping I was over the effects of the drug, for the past twenty minutes the effects seemed to have stopped. I tried to make my way back to the sleeping quarters when on my first step, I fell flat on my face. I wasn't laughing anymore, it seemed the effects went to my feet, they felt like I had one hundred pound weights on each foot. Picking up one foot at a time by grabbing and lifting up my thigh was the only way I could move. A very exhausting hundred yards later, I made it to my cot and was in dreamland in seconds. I never smoked pot again or did any other kind of drug for the rest of my tour in Vietnam.

Drugs became a big problem for the military in Vietnam as the years past, more so among the troops who were near large cities, where access to any kind of drug was much more prevalent. With many of our troops being drafted and the fact that it was an unpopular war, was enough for many of them to indulge in a variety of drugs. I can tell you, a lot of the people who became addicts extended their tours so they could have easy access to their drug of choice, which could be bought on the cheap. Personally, after my experience with the opium-laced pot, I found it hard to believe anyone would go out into the field and possible combat and do so while under the influence of anything.

One other point of interest about mess duty was the time we had a red alert. Red alerts were taken very seriously, even if the ones I went through were only drills. Thank God that was the only kind I had experienced on Hill 54. If it was for real, it meant we were being attacked. Well, if you were on mess duty your job was to get in the bunker for the mess duty people. The night we had this drill I noticed someone sneaking up to our bunker, dressed in black pajamas, the kind the V.C. wore. I knew almost immediately that it wasn't a V.C., but that it was most likely Captain [Buck] Darling, the C.O. of Company C. This man was a Marine who was respected by both the Officer Corps and the enlisted men, which he once was when he first became a Marine. He was so well known that Time Magazine did a story on him around 1967. I personally saw him in action when we were in a column moving up a mountain ridgeline. We started getting some light mortar rounds from a position a couple hundred yards ahead of us. When this happened, I was at point and brought the movement to a halt. Some officer moved up to my position and started to call up the mortar squad to respond. When Capt. Darling came up to our position, he borrowed a rifle from a Marine, fired three rounds in the direction of the bad guy and that was the end of any incoming rounds. I remember him saying to the other officer, "There's your mortar".

When I was sure it was the captain, I motioned the other guys in the bunker over to my position and filled them in on the situation. On cue, we all at once aimed our weapons at him yelling out "Who goes there?" I'm not sure if we scared him any, but after identifying himself, he did tell us, "Good job, Marines". Captain Darling was known to have snuck up on sleeping Marines who were on guard duty on an outpost, remove their rifle and leave a note in its place, telling it's owner to see him in the morning to get it back. Being on guard duty without a weapon, particularly guarding an outpost [a very scary thing to go through] was the lesson the captain got across to these individuals.

CHAPTER 25
GUARD DUTY – CHU LAI

Our next duty was guarding the Chu Lai airstrip and just like mess duty for the same reasons, it was considered good duty. Guarding the perimeter of the air base was our principal duty. It was duty not many complained about. The bunkers we stood guard in were strong enough to take a direct hit from a 155-millimeter artillery round. I didn't worry too much about that though. It would have been almost impossible for the enemy to get in range of the base without their being found out. As I mentioned before, from the center of the base you could fan out for thirty miles in any direction and you would run into Marines from Company strength on down. The enemy seemed to know better than to come into our patrolled areas!

It was a good time for me, much like the first time when I was here a few months back. I had plenty of time to catch up on a lot of unanswered letters. There sure was a collection of them. Most of the letters were from my father, who kept me abreast of what was happening at home and with the family. My aunt Alice, sister of my mother, who was a Wave during World War II and knew how much a letter meant, sent me nearly as many as my father. The rest of my immediate and extended family of relatives also added many more letters along with plenty of the coveted care packages they sent to me. I was very fortunate in this regard and I always shared part of the goodies with the rest of our squad. My next book will be all about those letters; I have them all, sent and received.

I guess the letters traded between Angel and me were at first typical, but as the time passed on, we seemed to argue more and more about what we hoped our future would be like once we were married. By the time I had spent five months in Vietnam, we were nowhere close on that subject and I suggested that we should end our relationship. Shortly after, we did.

Duty at the air base also had other advantages. One of them was the village that popped up shortly after the base went up. This village had just about everything a Marine might need for almost any activity. When you had the time off, you could also go to the beach and party. It's hard to believe we were able to do that in Vietnam. The air base at Chu Lai was also an in-country R&R center. With its beautiful beaches, it wasn't hard to see why it was made one. On the beach there were a couple of clubs, one for officers, and the other for enlisted soldiers. These clubs were not just for American troops, but also for any of our allies fighting there. One day while I was visiting the enlisted men's club, I got to meet and mingle with some South Korean Marines. When you talk about some bad dudes, then you are talking about these guys. Hanging around these guys made me think I was in a physical fitness center. It seemed anyone of them could take Tarzan's place and they weren't very lenient to anyone who screwed up either. One Korean Marine came into the club with a weapon, with a magazine inserted into it; this was something that was made very clear to anyone going into the club, not to do. Within seconds, the other Korean Marines in the club were all over that poor fool and beat the hell out of him. About an hour after that episode, a South Vietnamese soldier who thought he was a real bad dude came into the club and challenged anybody to try and fight him. I think he knew something about the martial arts, but not anywhere near what the

Korean Marine knew who beat his ass quite thoroughly. A tragic thing happened that day; a Marine who had three days to go before his tour was finished and was about to go home, got drunk, went swimming, and drowned.

CHAPTER 26
SHIT BIRD

There is a saying in the M.C. and that is, "In every M.C. outfit there will always be the 10% who don't pull their load." We were unfortunate to get one person who made up that 10% all by himself. He was the original gold-brick! The first indication that he fit into such a category was when he was transferred to us from another company. This normally didn't happen unless the person had special qualifications; he didn't. We got him because it's a good bet his life was in danger and not from the enemy. Another reason was the fact that he had a Purple Heart Medal that was not his; it turned out that it was stolen from some other guy from his last outfit. You must understand that stealing supplies from someone like the Army was an acceptable act, but stealing from a fellow Marine was about the worst thing you could do; you became despised and not trusted. But this man really gave us reason to wish he had never showed up.

Our squad had just come off guard duty. We were told to clean up our rifles for an inspection. Just as we were to be inspected we were told to oil our weapons down thoroughly. Then we were told why: our one and only "Shit Bird" was AWOL and we had to go out and find him. A late afternoon thunderstorm was putting out some heavy rain. Oiling our weapons was needed to prevent rust from forming. From all the grumbling going on in our squad, I

detected that they were feeling just as I was and that was-
"God help that bastard when I get my hands on him!"

We got a lead on his whereabouts from one of the local villagers. "Our" boy had found himself a girlfriend and decided he wanted to be with her instead of us. Her village was a couple of miles outside the base perimeter. It was a wet and muddy hike to that village and we were seeing red by the time we got there. We soon found out what hooch they were in and, as we were surrounding it, gave him sixty seconds to get his ass out of it. Lucky for him he did because I think he was real close to really getting messed up by us. We roughed him up a little but didn't hurt him; unfortunately, we were still stuck with him.

CHAPTER 27
LEAVING CHU LAI

As our one-month of duty guarding the airbase was coming to its conclusion, we couldn't help but see all the Army personnel moving onto the base. All of us were trying to figure out why they were. The main rumor floating around was the Army was moving in to replace all the Marines in the Chu Lai area. From all the supplies and equipment they were bringing on base, this seemed to be the case. Now the rumors started about where we were going next. The rumors and plain logic said we would be going up north somewhere. If this being the case then it meant we would be getting to tangle with the NVA [North Vietnam Army] regulars. I wasn't too sure I was glad to hear this possibility but I thought it would be better because you would at least finally get to see whom you were fighting. That was almost never the case with the V.C.

During our last week of guarding the airbase we finally got the word that we would indeed be moving up north. We were going to the Que Son Valley area. From what some of the "old salts" from the company were saying, we were in for some major nasty times in the near future. They should know because on Operation Colorado in August 1966 they encountered the NVA 3rd Regiment in the Que Son Valley and had a fierce battle with them and managed to kill over a hundred of that unit.

Now knowing that we were going up north, we knew

we were going to be out in the field living off "C" rations for some time. If you never had C-rats before, well let me tell you, C-rats at their best are like a left over meal that was bad to start with. We couldn't believe the amount of C-rats the Army had brought onto the base. They literally filled a square block eight feet high with them. Now some C-rats can be made somewhat edible with hot sauce and some spices, but its best to have a good selection to pick from to ensure the best results. All we needed to do was get some of the Army's C-rats, problem solved. Knowing the Army was not going to give them to us, we had to figure out a way to take the C-rats from them. We used "Naked Strangle-Holds" on the two sentries guarding the C-rats. Used properly, the hold first silences the sentry and depending on the amount of time and pressure used, either knocks him out or kills him. Of course we only knocked out the sentries then gagged and tied them up. With that done, we brought in a two-ton truck and loaded it in record time. It would have been great to be around when the Army brass found out about our little escapade. We weren't done yet though, you see, we also realized that the Army had brought on base a very large supply of beer. This beer was kept in a big tent in the Army's headquarter section on the base. To get to this beer, we decided a distraction would be the way to go in this case. Two of us started fighting in front of the tent and sure enough, it got a whole lot of attention from all the Army personnel in the area, including the guys in the beer tent. Once the tent was clear of the Army guys, we pulled a jeep up to the back of the tent, cut a slit down it and filled the jeep up in no time and were out of there. A signal was given to the Marines fighting each other and they just faded away into the crowd. Enjoying the fruits of our labor made the prospect of our future somewhat easier on all of us.

Hill 54, my home for five months. Happy Valley is on the other side of the mountains in the background.

Base Mess Hall on Hill 54, spent two months working in this building.

The Church on Hill 54 that was used by all religious faiths.

This is one of the hooches in the village outside the gates to Hill 54. This lady did my laundry and cooked meals for me.

My first squad leader, Sgt. Hollers, and me in our tent on Hill 54.

Me and the rest of our squad in our tent on Hill 54. That's "Fitts" waving.

Posing in some of my "Tunnel Rat" gear by a tank on Hill 54.

CHAPTER 28
THE MOVE UP NORTH

Upon returning back to our base hill 54, we were surprised at the activity going on all over the base. When we got to the area where our company was located, we found that the camp was being dismantled. All of our personal gear except our field gear was already packed up and put in storage somewhere. The tents we lived in were down and stored, leaving just the wood floor shells of the tents still in place.

Within fifteen minutes after returning back to our quarters, our squad was issued ammo and told to take a patrol out north of the base where we had gone so many times before. Unlike all of the patrols of the past where we never encountered resistance, this patrol found some. It seemed our enemy was aware of what was going on and were moving closer to our base. I believe during the process of the Army moving in and the Marines moving out, the long and short range patrols we used to conduct were not being taken over by the Army, allowing the enemy the chance to get close enough to reconnoiter the situation and react. After traveling about halfway to our destination we stopped for a break. Within just a couple of minutes, our squad started to receive fire from two different locations. We couldn't believe it; getting fired on had never happened so close to our base before. This proved to be quite a dilemma for us because we weren't where we should have been; hence we couldn't rely on any support from the battalion. Knowing this, our squad leader told us to move out double time to the area we were supposed to be. It didn't take much motivation for us to get moving in that direction. Running for several hundred meters, we came up to a good size rice paddy where we knew Highway 1 was on the other side of. Figuring that we would be safer on that side, our squad leader told us to start moving across the paddies as fast as we could. In the process, we saw some Vietnamese people who seemed out of character. As we got closer they started to run from us. Our squad leader fired his M-79 grenade launcher, landing a round about 25 meters in front of them. They all dove to the ground when the round went off. When I was coming up on this one guy, he was starting to get up and was turning towards me when I caught him across the jaw with the butt of my M-16, knocking him back to the ground. He dropped a mean looking knife as he went down, one that I was sure he would have tried using on me. With these people in tow, we continued moving across the paddies when we started receiving 50 cal. machine gun fires from the same spot where we entered these paddies. These rounds were splashing up rice paddy water some twenty feet in the air, all too close to us. There was what looked like some kind of cover about a hundred meters in front of us, but a herd of water buffalo was between that spot and us. We were running and screaming at them in an attempt to get them out of the way; they moved just before we were going to blow them away. Part of the squad got to the covered area and put some fire into the machine gun position; they either hit them or they decided to call it a day because that was the last of their fire.

Once we got across the rice paddies and were on Highway 1, we called into the base telling them of our possible V.C. suspects. Glad to hear the orders to head back to the base, we gathered up our suspects and moved out. Once back on the base, we turned them over and rejoined our unit that was staging up on Highway 1. Shortly afterwards, the truck transportation started to show up and company by company we were trucked up to an area just outside the city of Tam Ky which was about eight miles north of Hill 54 on Highway 1. As our battalion was moving out, an Army battalion was replacing us on our old home, Hill 54.

Outside our temporary base at Tam Ky, the Army had set up an artillery base that our company was temporally going to guard. After setting up our defensive positions, we settled in for about a week. The week went by pretty quiet and uneventful. Except for the occasional artillery mission being fired, our time there was pretty boring. One thing did happen that was quite funny. The company was called together for a meeting. With his back to the artillery, the company gunnery sergeant was filling us in on what was going on. At the same time, the Army's M107's, a 175mm gun was preparing to fire. This was the biggest land gun in that war; it had a range of thirty-three kilometers; when they fired they did so with one hell of a bang. The gunny sergeant didn't notice the guns preparing to fire and when they did fire he hit the deck faster that anyone I had ever seen do so before now. All of us including the gunny got a good laugh out of it. During the gunny's talk to us, we learned the rumors were true. As of April 25, 1967, we were part of a division size operation called UNION.

CHAPTER 29
OPERATION UNION

Our mission was to eliminate the 2nd Division of the NVA. This division had been in the Quang Tin and adjacent Quang Nam Provinces for many, many years. This meant to us that the local village people were more likely to sympathize with the NVA than they would with us. We knew this was going to make our time there all that much more difficult.

Within a couple of days from the start of the operation, a company from our battalion engaged elements of the 21st North Vietnamese Regiment in the La Nga-2 area. With this contact over the next week, the rest of the 5th Marine Regiment was put into the field to pursue the 21st Regiment. Our company was lifted out by helicopter to an area near La Nag-2. The first couple of days out in the field went by without many incidents. At the end of the third day, our company stopped and set up our defensive positions. We all dug in deep and set up our lines of fire before settling in for the night. It wasn't very long after this that the silence of the night was broken. Our company had set up in a circle about 100 meters in diameter. From areas all around us, we started receiving rifle and light mortar fire. We retaliated with our own rifle and mortar fire. This went on for an hour or so when the enemy broke it off. The next morning, upon inspecting the outside of our perimeter lines, we found some blood but no dead enemy. It was thought that it was a unit checking out our strengths. No one got hit that night. When we pulled out the next morning, our one and only "Shit-bird" was put into the point position. This person had no business being put in this position and sure enough after moving about a quarter of a mile, an enemy sniper fired one shot and put the round right between his eyes. A lot of us felt badly about this happening, particularly me, because I been at the point position from the beginning of this operation. Even though he may have been considered a "Shit-bird", he still was a Marine. Later on we learned he was trying to get out of Vietnam on a hardship discharge. This was a discharge given to Marines that had serious problems at home, such as a parent dying, etc. This may have been why he was a "Shit-bird" in the first place, but I guess we will never know. It seemed that the sniper had only him in his sights that day because that one shot was the last shot we received from the enemy. The company didn't travel much further that day. It took awhile to clear an opening so a helicopter could come in to remove the dead body of shit bird. Heavy jungle terrain and lack of paths was slowing us down quite a bit. As the terrain started to get more mountainous, we stopped for the day and dug in for the night. Several squads from the company were sent out to reconnoiter the surrounding area. I was running point for our squad when we came upon a path. After following the path for a bit, I came across signs indicating enemy presence in the area, possibly an ambush or booby traps. As I moved further along this path, I stopped the squad when I came up to a 40 by 50 foot clearing. Every sense in my body was telling me that this was an ambush. The squad moved into counter positions and once they were set up, I started to enter the clearing. I was about a third of the way into the clearing when they opened up on us. I fell to the ground and played like I was dead, considering there was no kind of cover at all for me other than trying to get out of the clearing into the most likely booby- trapped jungle. Playing

"Possum" seemed the right thing to do. Like in a slow motion movie, I watched a line of machine gun fire coming right at me. Just when I thought I was going to get hit, my squad leader, as planned, put an M-79 round in the machine gunner's lap, killing him and keeping me alive and not a second too soon. The rest of the squad killed the other two members of this ambush. We radioed to the company what just happened to us and were told to get back to the company area. All of us were happy to oblige. Later that night, I was told I was now a Lance Corporal and a Fire Team Leader. I guessed by now my immediate superiors thought I was due for a promotion, considering I was doing most of the "Tunnel Rat" jobs that were coming up and running "Point", mainly because I liked doing those jobs. I accepted my promotion graciously.

The next morning we woke up to orders to saddle-up and to move out double-time. Charley Company from our battalion was getting hit real badly. Their company was about 5 miles away on top of hill 110. They were receiving heavy fire from caves that were located in a higher mountain near them and from a cane field below and were taking a lot of casualties. Moving out was slow going; we were in a triple canopy jungle moving up steep mountains. When I couldn't find streambeds or animal paths to use, I had to cut a path. It also had to be the hottest place I had to endure up to that point in my tour. The company had 38 Marines that had come down with either heat stroke or heat exhaustion making this trip. By the time we got to Charley Company, it was far too late. It was horrible; it was like seeing the surface of the moon, with craters from all the incoming rounds all over the top of Hill 110. Dead bodies or parts of them were strewn all over the place. It must have been terrifying for them. Air strikes and our artillery had silenced the enemy for now. Unfortunately, Alpha Company from our battalion, who were also trying to get to Charley Company's position from another direction, was mistakenly hit with some of our own air power. Five Marines were killed along with 24 Marines getting wounded. We tended to the dead and wounded of Charley Company and then started down the other side of the mountain we had just come up. It was quite a contrast to the jungle we just came out of. The land was flat and clear for as far as you could see, but it was hot, very hot. Once we got down the mountain, we found a well. Since we had gone now for over two days without finding water we were very glad to find this well. We were very skeptical though about using it, for there were 35 dead bodies lying all around the vicinity of the well. We believe they were "Red Chinese," because they looked very different from the Vietnamese we normally saw and because of all the propaganda we found on and around them, made us think that much more that they were Chinese. One of the pieces of propaganda I found on them went like this. "Escalators can go up or down but Johnson's escalator can go only one way and that's down, down into a rough pine box." On the other side of this propaganda leaflet was a scene of a burial ceremony at Arlington National Cemetery. It seemed ironic to me that it was the propagandists with this material that were the ones dead. For the first time since I've been in this country, I got sick to my stomach. A bunch of us were told to search the bodies for identification or weapons. As I grabbed the foot of one of the propagandist to turn him over, the skin from his knee on down to the top of his foot, fell down to his ankle like a loose fitting sock. These people had been dead for quite awhile and between the stench and this guy's skin falling down, well; it was enough for me to throw up. I didn't search any more bodies that day. We checked the well out and it seemed OK. The whole company filled-up their canteens from the well, most of us put in our water purifying tablets, but not all of us including me. I wished I had, because a few days later, several other Marines and I came down with diarrhea something awful. It was so bad that I went with no underwear and slit my pants in the crouch area so all I had to do was stop, spread my legs and go; all that came out of me was nearly liquid. I eventually lost about 45 pounds because of my stupidity.

Our next objective was a small hill that overlooked a river that was about three miles into this beautiful valley. Upon arriving at this hill, which was to become our temporary base, we were assigned to the areas we were to defend and we dug in. After what we saw of Charley Company's encounter with the NVA, we were starting to gain a healthy respect for the NVA. All of us dug our foxholes a lot deeper that day and did so without being told to do it. That night passed without any incidents to report and in the morning we all took turns swimming in the river. This was the first time any of us got to wash ourselves since the beginning of this operation. To say the least, it was immensely appreciated. Swimming in the river had one disadvantage and that was the leaches. These blood-sucking creatures were everywhere in Vietnam. On one particular patrol while we were moving through area that was full of elephant-grass, we stopped for a break. I was sitting down in this small clearing eating some C-rat peaches when I notice that from all directions around me were hundreds of leaches moving in my direction. After one of my swims in the river I removed 39 leaches that attached themselves on my body.

From our temporary base, we went out on platoon-size patrols to reconnoiter the area. Not much came about from these patrols; there were very few indications that the NVA or the V.C. were anywhere in the area. When we would return to the temporary base, we would work on our positions and equipment, catch-up on letters and when the chance came, take a few dips in the river. After a week or so at this base, new fresh troops started moving in with us, helping to reinforce the base.

CHAPTER 30
MAIL CALL

Olivia, I would like you to read the letter I received from my father about this time in my tour in Vietnam:

May 15, 1967
Dear Paul:

We have not heard from you for over two weeks now and we know that that means only one thing, you have been traveling up in Happy Valley. We read in the papers and hear on the radio that the 5th Marines are in heavy action between Tam Ky and Hoi An and from the picture you sent of Happy Valley I would take it that is just about where it is located. Well, wherever you are we are praying for you and asking God to bring you through unscathed. I am mailing you a package today and since I did not hear from you about any new things you might want you are getting the same old assortment including a new can of bug juice. I can just imagine the animal life in that jungle at 130 degrees. I hope the stuff keeps them at bay. We also read a couple of stories about tigers stalking troops on patrol. There was a picture in the paper of a couple of GIs who had bagged one together with the dead tiger. But with all the noise in a big operation the tigers probably go looking for a place to hide. Mothers Day was yesterday and we insisted that mother have her breakfast in bed. She loved it but I am sure that she would have been much happier if you were home here with her to celebrate. Next year should be a happy one. One of the Farrington boys was killed in South Vietnam. I think it was Buddy. He had been drafted into the Army and had been over there only for about a month. Your mother and Sue went to see him laid out and said that he looked pretty bad. They laid him out with his hat on. He apparently had been hit in the head.

Your Aunt Feenie is still in the hospital. Her heart condition was a little more serious than we thought at first and we have decided to keep her in the hospital for a while until she is completely better. I don't know whether they have told Michael so don't mention it to him if you have the have the chance to write him. I could have the Red Cross bring him home on leave but he would have to go back and make up the time he was away from VN so since his mother is really not that bad I think it would only make it worse for her when he had to go back. What do you think about a situation like this? Do you think that it is better this way or do you think it would be a good idea to get a leave for him? Let me know whenever you get the chance.

You had asked me about your high school diploma in one of your other letters and I had forgotten to answer you before. I had called Cheltenham H.S. about it and they gave me some story about you owing them some money for books and they said that they could not issue the diploma until this was taken care of. This is no problem but I was just wondering if you knew anything about it. The person I talked to did not seem to know any details except that there was a charge against you on the books and she thought that it was probably for some books that you did not return when you left to join the Corps.

I am enclosing in this letter the pictures that you requested. There is a dozen. You must have quite a fan club over there. Are you autographing them before you give them out? There is also enclosed a copy of a prayer. I think it is the same one you have with you but every little bit helps. It was given to me for you by a patient, Mrs. Margaret Haley, 2809 N. Howard St, Phila Pa. 19133. You might drop her a letter note thanking her if you get the time. There are also some scapulars. Give the extra ones to some of the other boys. They were given to me for you by Mrs. Mary Jonas, 3429 N. Bodine St. Phila Pa. 19140. Her husband was a Marine in the South Pacific in WW II and her three sons have also been Marines. One of them was in Korea but the other two were in during peacetime after Korea. Your mother just came in from the store and she just heard more bad news on the radio. They said that the fighting where we think you are is so bad that the Marines were using tanks to bring out the dead and wounded and that they were refusing to give out the number of casualties until the action is over. She is pretty much upset but I told her that all we can do is keep on praying. So write just as soon as you can, even if it is just one line to let her know that you are all right.

The weather here has been horrible for the past three weeks. It has been raining almost every day. Liz wrote us and said that it has been the same out in Ohio. Everybody is getting anxious now that school is drawing to a close. They are all talking about the shore for the summer. Liz will be down with us for a couple of weeks before she takes off for Europe. Sue has decided that she would like to go back to Brown County next year so by September there will be three away, you and the two girls. It is just possible also that Jack might be gone. They are talking about calling up the Reserves and if they do he will go. I don't think they would take Michael on Active duty because of his bad knee but you never can tell if things begin to really get bad and from the way it looks it will be a lot worse before it gets better. Tommy is still in Temple and apparently they are going to continue to defer all college students and apparently he has studied enough to make it into his sophomore year. That is something you must think about when you get back. You will have your HS diploma and with the GI bill paying your way plus giving you $150.00 per month you would be extremely foolish not to go back to college. I am sure you can get into college. You would not have to take any very hard courses but you should get a college degree. Jack is finding out that without one it is pretty nearly impossible to get a really good job even though he has three years of college. He is still working for Honeywell but if he had his degree he could be working for another company in a much better job paying up to $10,000 per year, and they don't ask whether the degree is in philosophy or dance appreciation just so that you have a degree. So think it over. The time goes very quickly and an opportunity like this, that is, the GI bill, should not be lost. Remember I was 25 when I went back to college and even though it seemed like a long time to go when I made that decision, now it seems that it was only a few days before I was graduated from Medical School. You have a long life ahead of you and after what you are going through over there you should make the best of it.

But now the time has come for me to go to the office so I will say good-bye and God bless you until we see you again in the fall.

Dad

Mail call was generally the highpoint for most of us in the field; I know I always looked forward to it. I'll give you some more information to complete my father's letter to me. Aunt Feenie was my Cousin Mike's mom, who was married to my dad's brother. I advised my father not to tell Mike anything about his mom's condition. If he knew about it, he would have that on his mind and that could get him killed. It turned out that my aunt did have a relapse and, according to my instructions, my cousin Mike was back at her side within 24 hours. This became possible when a friend of my father, Congressmen Jimmy Burns, cut through the red tape and had my cousin pulled out from the field and put on a plane home. Aunt Feenie died the day after Mike got back. He never went back to Vietnam and got a Hardship discharge out of the M.C.

My father's patients lived primarily in the Kensington section of Philadelphia, the same part of town my father grew up in. I'm sure you saw the "Rocky Balboa" movies and remember the pet shop that Adrian worked in. Well that shop was on Front St. and my father's office was directly across from it. The prayer that one of my father's patients sent me was the same one I already carried with me all the time, more on that later on in this story. I also sent these patients thank you notes for thinking about me in their prayers.

I tried answering all the letters that were sent to me. Many were from people I had never met, from whole classes of grade school children and from friends of both my brothers and sisters. For the life of me, I can't think of why I wanted my father to send me some pictures of myself, maybe to send to Mimi Ma. Also, when I went through boot camp, I took the GED test and passed it. I wanted my father to find out if I would be able to get a diploma from Cheltenham High School. A bit further on in this story I'll show you the last letter I got from my father.

On May 5th Delta Company went out on a long-range

patrol. With the weather being on the good side for once, we found moving through the dry, open valley easy going. Several hours out on this patrol, we came to a halt to take a break and have some C-Rats for lunch. My platoon sergeant told me to go on about a half-mile or so further to check things out. By this time in my tour in Vietnam, I had become very comfortable in being the "Point Man" for our company. As I mentioned before, I had a great teacher, Big John. I felt good about myself that my platoon sergeant thought I was ready for the responsibility that came with this position. I went out about half a mile or so and all that was to be seen was the incredible beauty of this valley. I didn't even see any of the local villagers out in the rice paddies or on the road I was on and didn't quite understand why. I headed on back to the company. Once I got back, I went looking for my platoon sergeant. I found him in a circle on the dirt road we had been following, with the other platoon sergeants and officers, who were working on our next move. My platoon sergeant was thumping the road with his walking stick that he always carried to the field, while he was down on one knee. To me it didn't sound right, it sounded sort of hollow to me. This immediately made me suspicious and I made my concern known to him as calmly as I could. When I did this, I watched my platoon sergeant turn pale white right in front of me. After taking a moment to gather his self, he very calmly told all the Marines sitting down on the road to very slowly move backwards off the road. About fifteen minute's later, we had cleared away enough of the hard packed earth that was covering most of the area where they were sitting around to expose about a six foot long, three foot wide, five foot deep hole. In the hole, there were about twenty-five punji stakes, usually made from bamboo whose ends sticking up were sharpened to a point. This particular pit was so old that if someone had fallen in, the bamboo most likely would have crumbled instead of sticking. But if it was a fresh one; god help him, even if he survived the sharpened punji stakes, he had a good chance of getting blown away by a booby-trapped grenade that a moved punji stake would release. It was a no-win situation and one you hoped you never had to experience. This was the first "Man Trap" I had seen and I hoped my last.

Shortly after this incident, we prepared to move out. This time we stayed off the road. The company had traveled several miles when we came up to this river, the Song Chang; I believe it was the same river that flowed by our temporary base. The orders were to split up the company, with half the company going to the other side of the river and the other half staying on this side, then move out following the river upstream. I was part of the company to cross the river. I found a spot that I thought might be all right and started crossing; I wasn't even half way when I realized that this was not a good place to cross. The water was just too deep for a good crossing. Since I was nearly completely soaked I decided to continue on across anyway. As the water got deeper, I raised my rifle up over my head to keep it dry. The water was getting deeper and before long all you could see of me was the very top of my helmet and my two arms sticking out of the water holding up my rifle. Much to my relief, the water started getting shallower and before long I was out of the water and on the other side of the river. I guess I must have looked kind of funny to these guys, because they all seemed to get a kick out of my crossing. The rest of the company decided to find a better crossing further up the river. They didn't have far to go, within less than a hundred yards they found a much better crossing, so good most of the guys crossing hardly got their boots wet. I got quite a ribbing about my choice of crossings. Hey, what can I say, it was a hot day anyway; I was dry within a very short period of time.

As we continued up the river, the banks along it started getting higher and thicker. Not much further up the river, I started to find pens, about 10 feet by 10 feet in size, dug out of these embankments. The pens were used to hold water buffalo. The first ones I came across were empty. A bit further up, I was looking away from the embankments as I came upon another pen. The loud snort of a water buffalo alerted me to the fact that this pen was not empty and I managed to turn around in time to unload a full clip from my M-16 into the charging beast. A second later, I might have been lifted to new heights or stomped into oblivion. The water buffalo was the peasant farmer's tractor, without it he couldn't survive. Before long, the water buffalo in this area became fair game for the slightest provocation. As we continued further up the river, we discovered an NVA camp. It was abandoned but not that long ago from the looks of it. The camp was a fairly large one, with an extensive tunnel system. In the tunnels we found a large cache of supplies that could support at least a regiment. The supplies consisted of food, medical items, uniforms and ammo, but no weapons. Most of the supplies were blown up where we found them in the tunnels along with the tunnel system itself. The food, which was not in the tunnels, was burned in place. Once we were sure the camp was destroyed, the company headed on back to the new base. A few days after returning back to the base, we were moved off again to replace Bravo Company of our battalion who were guarding a new artillery base that was being set up. Upon arrival at this new base, it was very obvious to all of us that a war was going here. I asked one Marine from Bravo Company what was going on and why did they dig their foxholes so deep. He very seriously answered, "If I were you, I would dig them deeper, for the last three nights we were getting hit with heavy mortars. God help you." I heeded the advice; our foxhole was nearly 10-11 feet deep when the mortars started that night. Being on the receiving end of a mortar or worse yet, an artillery attack is one of the most unbelievable, frightening experiences anyone could go through. I was quite beside myself, when one mortar round landed close to our foxhole, knocking part of it on top of me and the other Marines in it. What really gets to you during a mortar or artillery attack is that you are totally defenseless against it. You couldn't personally fight it; you just had to sit there and take it while sitting in your foxhole or better yet, a reinforced bunker and praying that none of the incoming rounds had your name on it.

In the beginning of the mortar attack that night, we were receiving about 30 incoming rounds from 82 MM mortars a minute, for a good 15 minutes we were getting hit with this rain of mortars. It was only after we were able to pinpoint the locations of the several NVA mortar teams firing on us that we were able to take them out of action. Each night the NVA mortar teams set up in different locations than the night before, which made it difficult to put a permanent end to their attacks on the base. After about an hour the incoming rounds finally stopped and a lot of us thanked God that they did. Word was passed around that night that we would be moving out in the morning. We were leaving our temporary base and moving to a new area to build a permanent base. The other companies from our battalion were to join us during the night and early morning hours for a battalion movement to this new area.

CHAPTER 31
MAY 12, 1967

About 0900, May 12, 1967 the Battalion had formed and moved out for our new destination. Delta Company was to bring up the rear of the movement, which meant that we would be following the battalion a few miles behind it. It was nearly three hours after we had moved out when word was passed up to me to come to a halt. A few minutes later my platoon sergeant came up to my position to tell me, "Mac, I want you to keep following this trail until you come to a major trail going off to your left. Follow that trail till you come to a village; it should be off to your right. Get on the trail that goes to the village, once you are on it, set your compass at a 110 azimuth and follow it. You get all that?" I repeated back to him what he told me and moved out for our objective. The trail going to my left wasn't much further down the trail I was on and I made the turn onto it. After traveling about two miles on this trail, some movement to my left caught my attention. I and my main man and best friend, Peterson, who was learning the "Point" business from me, went to take a better look of what was going on. As we approached this area, we saw two Vietnamese starting to run basically in the same direction that we were heading, Peterson and I took off after them, with Peterson taking the lead. The land that we were on was pretty clear of any obstacles, just some scrub brush. Peterson caught up with them and shot both of them. One of them was still alive when I finally caught up to them. Peterson screamed at me, "What took you so long!" I tried to explain that I was losing clips to my new M-16 rifle out of the ill conceived, makeshift pouch I was using to carry them in. I don't like to make excuses, but we were just issued these new weapons, but not the pouches for the clips. The pouches we did have for the M-14 rifle were way too big for these much smaller clips used in the M-16. So I did what every other Marine did and that was "IMPROVISE". Only problem was my improvising didn't work very well when you were running, as I was trying to explain to Peterson when the rest of the company caught up to us.

When the company commander [CO] got up to our position, he commenced to chew us out but good. "You idiots, you could have walked right into an ambush and got yourselves killed. From here on out, you don't do anything till I know about it; do you understand me? Of course we said, YES SIR! The CO then took a look at the Vietnamese that was still alive. One of the corpsmen was looking over him and explained to the CO, "Sir, this guy has two entry wounds in his belly but no exit wounds coming out, what you think happened sir?" "Don't know and I don't care, let's get the show on the road. Mac, you keep an eye open for that trail going to the village and set a course at 110 azimuths on your compass. You got that." "Yes sir, a 110 azimuth on the trail going to the village, got it sir."

When the CO went on back to his position in the column, the corpsman called Peterson and me over to where he was. He was giving the Vietnamese that was still alive an overdose of morphine to put him out of his misery. He said, "Man would you look at that, this guy has a hard-on. Man, this guy is going to his maker feeling beaucoup good." He did die with a smile on his face; about a minute later he was dead. I think this particular corpsman had a bit of a morbid side when he asked, "You guys ever see what an M-16 round can do to you when you get hit like this guy here? Well you're about to." He got out a scalpel and cut open this guys gut from the bottom of his belly to up his sternum and said, "Well will you look at that, this poor fool's insides are completely flipped around; it's like his innards went through a washing machine. I just can't believe he lived as long as he did." With that said, Peterson and I went on back to our position at the front of the column, waiting for the word to move out. I had a strong feeling that all hell was about to break out. We probably didn't go another quarter of a mile when I came up to the trail I was looking for. The village was only a few hundred yards down this trail. This village was in the hamlet of Phoc Duc. I took the right onto the trail and got out my compass and set it at a 110 azimuth and started following it. It set me in a direction that would veer to the right of the village. I probably went about 200 yards when I came up to this open area. The village was about 100 yards to my left. Out in front of me was an open field, maybe 200 yards wide and a hundred yards deep. It went up a 30-degree incline to a group of trees that was about 50 yards across. Other than some erosion grooves on this incline, it was void of any other cover whatsoever. On the far right side of this opening, I got to see my first NVA soldiers. It seemed like we caught the NVA off guard because they were scurrying all over that area, which made me now believe the two guys we ran down just a half hour earlier were most likely local V.C. on an outpost that we caught off guard. Because Peterson only fired four rounds killing them, it most likely was thought as some kind of horseplay and not much thought was given to it by NVA soldiers, who I'm sure, heard those rounds go off.

I had brought the column to a halt and asked the CO to come up to my position. He was there in no time. I said, "Sir, do you see what I'm seeing? Sir, a 110 azimuth runs right up the middle of this field to those trees. Are you sure you want me to go that way?" He said, "Hold on while I contact the battalion headquarters." From what I could hear of the conversation, the battalion commander didn't like his orders questioned. I could hear him screaming at the CO, "You got your orders, now follow them. You will be getting support from the rest of the battalion." What we didn't know at the time was that we were going to need all the support we could get. The NVA that I saw were part of an estimated two reinforced battalions of the 21st NVA regiment. The CO looked at me and said, "I believe you just heard the orders. Now get ready to move up to that tree line." Within a minute I started up the incline, following as much of the gouges in the soil that were created from erosion as I could, hoping the gouges would offer some kind of cover for the rest of the company. As I started up, I noticed a young healthy Vietnamese male walking in the same direction as I was. Even though he was not in a uniform and didn't have a weapon on him, I was sure he was an NVA soldier. He was about 25 yards to my right front and heading for the same trees as I was. I thought this guy had a lot of guts, walking out in the open like this. When he started running the last 10 yards to enter the trees, I opened fire on him. I wasn't sure if I had hit him or if it was his own motion to cause him to fly through the air the last few yards into the trees. All I do know is that when I fired on him all hell broke-out from my front and to the right side of me. This was a well thought-out "L" shaped ambush and here we were walking right into the jaws of it. The whole area busted loose with gunfire and mortar rounds going off all around us. All of the company hit the deck and returned fire at the NVA soldiers. Up front where our platoon was positioned, we were receiving heavy automatic machine gun fires from the trees. In response our platoon sergeant ordered McKinley's squad to move to the right and try a flanking maneuver into the right side of the trees. The squad never had a chance, only two of the twelve Marines in McKinley's squad made it back to where the rest of us were. They walked into about 50 well-entrenched NVA soldiers who were waiting on them. McKinley was the only one of the two Marines who managed to get back unharmed. The other Marine was not so lucky, as he was badly wounded.

I liked McKinley; he was my first fire-team leader who gave me some good advice on how to survive my tour in Vietnam, such as, "When we are in the field, watch me and do exactly what I tell you when you are told to do something. Keep your weapon clean enough that you can eat off it. The weather over here can turn your weapon into shit in a day, so keep it well oiled in the field. If you make it through your first combat in one piece, you might survive your tour over here." He cared a lot about his men.

To my left, I noticed four Vietnamese dressed all in black, moving low towards the trees. I opened fire on them, but I wasn't sure if I hit any of them. I decided to get closer to the left side of the trees to see if I could see them. After getting to the base of the trees, which offered some protection for me, I decided to see if I could move more to the left and fight them from a flanking position or maybe even get into their lines from the left side of the trees. As I started moving in that direction, I noticed what looked like the silhouette of someone amongst the shrubs about 25 feet to my front. I squeezed off one round at it. Whatever it was, it was still in the same position as I moved up to it. It turned out that I shot a gravestone dead in its middle, which made me feel somewhat better. I moved almost to the end of the trees when I noticed a trench about 35 feet further out from the trees. It looked like it was as long as the width of the left side of tree line itself. I figured that it would be a good place for me to put some fire into their left flank and part of the front portion of the tree line where I could put some rounds into their front lines from an angle. I should mention that this clump of trees was in actuality a cemetery that was about 30 by 50 yards in size.

This may sound a bit weird, but nearly a year earlier to that day, I began having a recurring dream over a two-week period of time. In this dream, it was always about a combat situation and it always had this trench in it. When I first saw this trench that day, it was like I flashed back and was in one of those dreams. This, believe it or not, made me feel good because in the dreams I only get wounded, seventeen times, mind you, but lived. With this new surge of confidence, I was ready to make my move to get to that trench, but before I did, I decided to go into the trees on my belly near the end of the tree line [or cemetery if you prefer because that was what it was] to reconnoiter the area and see if I could possibly sneak up on one of these bastards. I had a problem though; I still had my noisy improvised pouch to hold all my clips for my M-16 rifle. To prevent me from giving my position away, I stuffed as many clips as I could into my pants and shirt pockets and web belt. Then I hid the rest of the clips in the pouch near the edge of the cemetery where I went into it. I went in about half way and didn't see anything so I turned and moved to the left edge of the cemetery where I could see the trench clearly and ran for it as fast as I could move.

According to "Fits", my squad leader, I was one very lucky Marine; he could have sworn that I was a dead man from all the automatic fire he said I received while making my way to that trench. He told me that he could barely see me for all the dirt and debris being kicked up from their fire. To be honest, I never realized that I was being fired at while making that trip. What did occur to me while making this trip was that the possible V.C. I fired on earlier might be in that trench, which I jumped into, ready to blow them away if they were. It turned out that the trench was empty. Once in it, I tried using an old trick that I learned from an old war movie I had watched in my pre-Marine Corps years. It involved trying to make the enemy think that there were more us in the trench than there really were. I extended the bipod on the end of my M-16 and put it over the top of the trench aimed at the tree line, realizing by doing so, I could put fire just above the base of the tree line and not have to aim it by sight. I would squeeze off a three or four round burst of fire then move to another part of the trench and do it again. I kept this up till I was down to my last clip of ammo for my M-16. I guess what I was doing was having the desired results because they were doing their best trying to take me out of action by throwing hand grenades. They just didn't realize the fire they were receiving from me was coming from the trench and not the base of the tree line where most of their hand grenades were landing. By now, the remainder of our platoon had managed to fan out and was able to put a much heavier volume of firepower into their positions. When they stopped throwing grenades at me and our firepower was keeping them down low, I started making my move first back to the base of the cemetery and got around to the place I went in it. I went back in to get the pouch of ammo clips but couldn't find them where I had left them, which kind of spooked me. Then I couldn't believe my luck, two NVA soldiers were making their way to this part of the cemetery. They were walking in a low stooped position when I aimed in on the lead one's head. I wanted to fire only once, for I was afraid there were others around that I wasn't seeing and I didn't want to give my position away with more than one shot. As it turned out, it was only one shot my rifle was going to fire anyway. When I fired, I missed, I was off by a split second and the round probably singed his eyebrows. I knew I missed him because he didn't go down and because I could see the tracer round that I fired at him floating way out beyond him. Had I hit him, I wouldn't have seen the tracer. I immediately pulled the trigger again; that's when I realized my rifle had jammed. It would have been so easy to take them both out because they remained standing a good couple seconds more after I fired the first round. The lead guy seemed puzzled; I guess I might have been too if I just realized a round almost took off my head. They finally ducked down and were out of my vision. I decided it was time to get back to my lines and get another M-16 that worked.

I made my way back to our lines and was replenishing my ammo from a pile of it collected from dead or wounded and out of action Marines, and got myself an M-16 that wasn't jammed. I had already decided that I was going back to that trench and was making my move to do so when a mortar round went off nearby. The blast from the round knocked me back to our lines, knocking me out in the process. I wasn't out for long and I wasn't injured badly. Most of the stuff that hit me was bits of rock and dirt kicked up from the explosion of the mortar round, giving me some nicks and cuts, but nothing major to speak of. I guess someone else thought otherwise; because I was awarded the Purple Heart for those nicks and cuts. Not long after I regained consciousness, the word was passed up to our position to move to the village.

It was starting to get dark and the company was badly in need to consolidate what were left of it and the badly wounded needed evacuation for medical treatment. The village offered far more cover than what the open field afforded the company. All around this village were very large boulders that gave us some protection from at least direct rifle fire. As the company filtered back to the village, they were directed to locations that were exposed to the outside and did their best to cover these areas with what was left of them. While the rest of my platoon was making their way back, I decided to hold tight for a bit. I wanted to make sure none of the NVA soldiers were going to come out and pursue our men, but even more so, I wanted very badly to see some of the enemy one more time up close and blow the hell out of them. A few minutes or so after the last of the platoon had pulled back to the village; none of the NVA soldiers were coming out of the tree line. Deciding a couple of hand grenades sent their way would keep it that way, I pulled the pins on two grenades and threw them where I thought they might be. As the last of the two hand grenades was going off, I made my move for the village. It was nearly dark by now, but enough light for me to see what was going on around me. I managed to pick up several clips of ammo and a K-BAR knife dropped by other Marines on their way to the village. I can't say for sure, but I think they might have spotted me and were walking mortars on me when I realized the last two they fired had just landed between where I had come from and where I was now, some 50 yards away, so I started running as fast as I could go and then dove to the ground when I heard the thump of the third round being fired from its tube. Good thing I did, because it landed not all that far from where I thought it would, sparing me from getting hit with anything except another mild concussion. I stayed glued to the ground trying to give them the impression that they got me and was praying my acting was good enough. It apparently was, for no more mortars came my way.

While I was still on the ground and looking at the village, I noticed what looked like a small ambush going on. From the green tracer rounds that come out of the AK-47 used by the NVA, it looked liked a couple of NVA soldiers were trying to take out the last fringes of the company trying to make their way to the village. It was a very short ambush; the Marines already in the village silenced the NVA guns very quickly. It had become quite dark by now and I used the cover of it making my way to the village with no more problems. As I approached the entrance to the village, I made sure that they knew I was coming in, by yelling out, "Don't fire. It's McNally, I'm coming in!" As I made my way into the village, I started getting this kind of hero's welcome from my platoon sergeant on down to the men in my squad. They were talking about medals, promotions and such. I was eating it up because in the Marine Corps, one didn't get this kind of treatment very often. Frankly though, I wasn't too sure why, all I did in my mind was what anybody would do in that kind of situation. I did get another Meritorious Field Promotion to Corporal the next day and now my own squad to run. I was feeling pretty good about the promotion, but I also thought it was rather ironic that it took nearly two years to make Lance Corporal and just two months to make Corporal. I just hoped that I was up to the task and responsibilities I had just been given.

Our battle with the NVA didn't stop once we secured the village. The company got chewed-up real bad in the battle out in the open field; we had over 70 Marines who were either wounded or killed. The badly wounded needed to be evacuated to a hospital, which meant helicopters were going to be needed. In a clearing in the village a strobe light was set up for the helicopters to guide in on. It was the first time I saw one of these lights. I'm sure they were great for the helicopters to guide in on, but I was real concerned that every NVA soldier in the area was also being guided in on it too. The first helicopter got in and was loaded up and got out without any problems. The second one that came in was not so lucky. When it was on the ground being loaded with wounded Marines, a few NVA soldiers had managed somehow to infiltrate in close enough to open fire on it, killing the pilot and the door gunner. I was helping load a wounded Marine when this happened. As we were putting him in the helicopter, I saw rounds digging into his already wounded leg. He was the last Marine evacuated that night; the co-pilot lifted the helicopter out of there once we had him on board. As soon as the helicopter lifted off and was out of there, I turned my attention back to my fire team and our position in the defense of the village.

Before we moved out earlier that day on this movement, I had requested and received four claymore mines, one for each of us in my fire-team. The men weren't happy with having to carry an extra three and a half pounds on their packs, but as I told them, "If the situation should come up where they would need them, they'd be thanking me later." Just before the helicopters came-in, I went outside of our perimeter in the same area we came into the village from and set up the mines to cover an exposed opening. The claymore mine is a nasty device. It fires thousands of ball bearings out in an arc to its front and anything standing, up to 50 yards out in its path, could kiss it goodbye. As the second helicopter was lifting off, the NVA were making a frontal attack into the opening that I had mined. The claymores worked as advertised and they killed or wounded over fifty of the attacking NVA soldiers. The claymores probably had a lot to do with saving our butts that night, and they became standard issued equipment from that night on any time members of our company went to the field.

Some members of our company may argue that it was the support of the Army's big 175MM artillery guns that saved our butts that night and I know if I was on the receiving side of it I wouldn't want to hang around either. Just the sound that round made as it was traveling to its target was enough to scare you to death; sounded like a subway train was coming through the air at you. The artillery was taking out the positions the NVA held during that day on the right side and in the cemetery. When these rounds were landing just over a hundred yards from our positions, we actually bounced a bit off the ground. If they had come any closer to our positions, we could have been in their killing zone. After the artillery lifted, the NVA had deserted the area and the battle was over for that night.

I mentioned McKinley earlier and about how he lost most of his men and how much he cared for them. Well, shortly after he made sure that his remaining badly injured member of his squad was on the first helicopter and out of there, he sneaked out of the village and went back to where he lost his other men; I guess to see if anyone else might have survived. How he got by the attacking NVA soldiers that were heading for the village I'll never know, or survive the artillery barrage laid down by the Army, is beyond me. But survive he did, about twenty minutes after the artillery lifted McKinley could be heard yelling out his name and warning the Marines in the village that he was coming in. One look at him and you knew he didn't find any of his men alive. All he brought back with him were some of his comrades' dog tags. The anger and frustration he was feeling was distorting his face, eventually it all just turned to hate. McKinley was part of the original landing group of the 5th Marine Regiment that secured the Chu Lai area for the future air base. Most of his squad were also part of that group; they were all good friends of his and as they were with the rest of the old salts in the company. A feeling of hate was surfacing up in most of us. For one poor NVA soldier that was captured, this hatred came out. He was on the ground on his side with his hands and feet hogtied. It seemed every Marine that passed him that night took out their hatred by giving him a good kick. The next morning the NVA soldier was dead. Unfortunately, he wasn't the only one who died that night. When the NVA made their attack the previous night, one of them was able to get close enough to throw a hand grenade into the village, wounding one of our men. At the time, both he and the corpsman thought it was a superficial wound. Apparently, the wound was worse than what they thought, because the next morning when someone checked on him, they found that he had died during the night.

    As the company was waiting on helicopters to take out the dead and wounded, I joined up with a few other squads' checking-out the battlefield of the day before. It was hard to believe it was the same field. Large craters created from the artillery now replaced the cemetery, which now was nearly devoid of most of its trees and nearly the whole length of the right side of the field. I'll give the Army credit for some very accurate fire from their big guns; it was all on target. Later that day, we found out we were fighting soldiers of the 21st NVA Regiment. The 5th Marine Regiment had been chasing the 21st since the beginning of this operation and the 21st made their last stand in the Phoc Duc Hamlet.

Starting with our initial contact with them on May 12th, the battle went on for another three days as other companies from the 5th Marines fought them. This action against the 21st Regiment nearly put them out of business, at least for the time being.It was hard for me and I suppose most of the other Marines who fought this battle to sort out our feelings that morning. The combination of shock, frustration, and sorrow for our dead, hate for the NVA, gratefulness that we were still alive, wondering if we would be next, played havoc with our thoughts that morning.

What was left of our company was joined up with another company that arrived in the early morning hours. After a final checkout of the area, we moved out for our next objective. We had traveled only a few miles when we came up on another village. As we were approaching it, McKinley spotted a villager running away from the village and us. Bad move, it made him the enemy. With one shot he took him down, walked over to where he was and emptied his M-16 into him. Later on, after the body was dragged into the center of the village, I was walking by it with my machete in my hand, when one of the two Marines standing by it said, "Hey man, why don't you cut that bastard's head off?" This was not what I would wantonly do in most cases, but after considering that he was dead I thought why not. The first blow I sent to his neck missed and the blade of the machete ricocheted off his upper chest area, exposing a rack of his ribs. Like I said, this was not my bag. I dropped the machete and told them to get it back to me when they were done with it. Later on I saw the severed head on top of a bamboo pole in the middle of the village. I guess some kind of message was being sent here. You could cut the tension in the air with a knife. The village was as far as we were going that day; we worked on our positions and weapons most of the day and quietly prayed for a quiet night. As the sun rose the next morning after a peaceful night, we packed up our gear and moved out for our new base, Hill 51.

Once we got back to this new base, things loosened-up a little more for us. Combat engineers had set-up portable showers; giving us the first showers we had since the operation started. Considering what we smelled like, they were a very welcome addition.

Up to this point in Vietnam, I wasn't what you would call very religious, in that I didn't attend religious services when I could have. When a field service was being offered for our lost Marines, I attended it. I prayed for their souls and mine and my men. Throughout my tour in Vietnam, I carried several religious articles that were given to me from family and friends. One was a prayer I carried with me all the time, it was a prayer that was given to a Knight from the Pope of that time before he left on one of the Crusades. According to its legend, if you carried, read or heard this prayer, you couldn't die a sudden death, be poisoned, burned, be overrun, or captured in battle. It didn't say anything about being wounded though; figured I could live with that. I've become a firm believer that those religious articles I carried, and the power of the prayers said for me certainly had something to do with the fact that I'm still here today.

CHAPTER 32
FNG'S

Our Company during the next two weeks more or less took it easy on the base. It was a time to unwind, rest and recuperation. Fresh troops were being sent in to replace the Marines we lost. This was not an easy time for me, mainly because the replacement troops we were getting, for the most part, were right out of boot camp and had only the training they got in the basic infantry school and the jungle training they got at Camp Pendleton. By now I knew that these replacements were going to be more of a hindrance that an asset to us. You just couldn't expect someone to come to a country like this with just a few months of training and be expected to know what to do. I know because even with the countless hours I had in combat training prior to my tour and even my woodsman knowledge I learned growing up didn't prepare me for what I was to encounter when I first got here. You had to live it, breathe it and embrace it before you could feel comfortable fighting in this war and country. I felt bad for these Marines because if they encountered any action like we had recently, I didn't give the FNG'S much of a chance surviving it.

By now, I had learned that it didn't pay to get too close to any of these new guys; it hurt too much when they got wounded or killed. With my new men, I had only this to say, "When we are on a base like this one and your duties are done, I don't give a damn what you do, but when we are in the field, if I tell you to do something and you don't, I'll blow you away myself." This may seem like a hard way to treat these guys, but I figured until they themselves were baptized under fire and got a taste of what it was like, their chance of survival depended much more on what I told them to do than anything else.

I think now is the right time to read my father's last letter to me that I received from him while I was still in that country: May 25, 1967.

Dear Paul:

We finally got your letters after more than three weeks without any word. It was rather harrowing waiting to hear from you because we knew where you were and from the reports in the papers here it must have been pretty awful. They would not announce the casualties as they usually do because they had to hold them back for security reasons; we knew where you were because the papers announced that it was the Fifth Marines who were handling Operation Union. Nothing was really announced until about 3 days after the operation began, also for security reasons, and when they did finally announce anything they said that the casualties were so heavy in one area that they were bringing out the dead and wounded on tanks. The prayers are really working for you to come out of that one with only a scratch on the nose. Are you really going to take a Purple Heart for that? Ha! Ha!

From your second letter describing the march and ambush we got the idea that whoever was in charge was a new boy. I know that the Marines do not have any 90 day wonders like the Army had in WW II, so we were wondering just who was the CO. Was he a 2nd Looey or a Sgt. Or what? You really didn't say, but whoever he was, if he made it, I am sure that he will listen to an old hand the next time he gets some advice. We were extremely proud to hear that you were recommended for a battlefield promotion and especially the Bronze Star. That is really something. I certainly hope that it comes through. I am sure that not many Marines receive such an honor. This will certainly look great on your record in the Corps, and also in the future in civilian life.

On first hearing what you did it seems pretty scary but on second thought it was probably the only thing you could have done to save yourself and your men. I think it really proves the old adage that the best defense is a good offense and this is really the motto that you followed, get them before they get us. We especially liked your description of the way you did it, sneaking up from behind. Just about the same time your outfit was in Operation Union, there was a lot of action up near the DMZ and one night the TV told and showed one outfit charging head on into a fortified bunker, right into machine guns. Jack and Michael immediately said how stupid can you be to make an attack like that because most of the Marines making the attack were killed or wounded. It certainly would have made more sense to have gotten behind them in some way like you did. You accomplish the same objective without taking unnecessary casualties.

Have you been thinking of what you will do when you get back to civilian life? As I told you in one of my previous letters you should certainly think of education. You will be only 22 years old when you get out and that is still very young. Remember that I was twenty-five when I returned to college and I had to do 9 years: 4 college, 4 medical school and 1 Internship. It seemed like a lot before I started but it went so fast that now looking back it seems like only a few days. And it certainly was worth every minute of it, as I am sure you will agree. We were glad to hear that you liked the cookies even though they were banged up a bit. We will send you some more with the next package. You still did not say if there was anything special that you wanted so we will keep sending the same things until we hear differently. I read in one of the Medical Magazines that there has been an increase in the number of cases of Malaria. This was blamed on the fact that the boys were neglecting to take their pills. The Malaria mosquitoes are especially bad in the mountain and jungle areas like where you are operating now so make sure that you take yours. Some of the Malaria in Vietnam is especially severe and it can kill you just as easily as a VC bullet, except that it takes longer, so a word to the wise should be sufficient.

By the way I did not intimate that the girl you met in HK was anything but a very nice girl. I wondered just what she was who would give money to a stranger. Now I know. She apparently was someone whose family was well to do and she felt an obligation to share her ability to pay with someone she really liked, especially knowing that you were in the military and certainly not wealthy. The Orientals are a wonderful type of people as Father Joe often told us and I am glad that you are corresponding with this girl. I know many Orientals in the Medical Profession and I think highly of all of them. Perhaps, some day, you will go back to HK, since now you have a motive, more than just sightseeing, that is.

One more thing I want to tell you about. I have noticed that with each letter you write your ability to handle the language is better. You have developed a really good vocabulary, your spelling has greatly improved, your descriptions of things and events are really precise and accurate, your punctuation is good and in general your letters are worth reading from a literary standpoint. Keep up the good work. To me it is an indication of your innate intelligence and your ability to really make something out of yourself when you get home.

I am going over to see your Grandmother. She is well, and I am really going over to see your Aunt Alice. She is going to Expo 67 tomorrow. That is the World Fair being held in Montreal, Canada this year. She is going with Aunt Mary and her kids. I am going over to give her some money to get me a set of coins that they are issuing for the fair. I would like to go myself but since we are going down to the shore for most of the summer I can't make it.

Aunt Feenie is OK. She went home from the hospital today. She will have to take it easy for a while but I am sure that everything will be alright. What she needs most is to hear that the war is over and Michael is home safe and sound. This is what your own mother would like to hear also, but since it is not that way all we can do is keep praying and hope.

I will close now and get going, but your mother will be writing to you soon and telling you all the family gossip.

Keep praying and keep safe,
Dad

It was this particular letter from my father that has had a profound effect on my life, particularly when it comes to my desire to write. My father, for the most part, was the only person up to that time in my life who truly complimented me on any of my abilities or gave me the encouragement and belief that I was able to accomplish anything I put in my mind to do.

Some clarification is needed here pertaining to my father's letter to me. As far as to who I was referring to in my letter about who was running things and who gave to order to march into an "L" shaped ambush that my father was not clear about. It was Colonel Hilgartner, our Battalion Commander who yelled at my Company Commander, to follow his orders to follow a 110 azimuth up to the cemetery. Why we didn't use another method to attack this "L" shaped ambush is beyond me and that would include the use of air power and artillery before attacking. Maybe he didn't realize the number of NVA who were set up in this ambush or have knowledge of the layout of the combat field of action. Or maybe he just wanted all the credit for himself by not sharing any of it with the other elements of support available, making us basically targets to hold the enemy where they were till we received support from other units from our battalion. Those are my own personal feelings in this matter; there might have been a better way to fight this particular battle without sustaining the number of causalities we received.

When I returned to the village and received the congratulations from my platoon sergeant on down to the men in my fire-team for what I did in this battle, I thought that the medal they were talking about was the Bronze Star and not the Silver Star that I was awarded four and a half months later. My brother Jack was under the impression that I received both the Bronze and the Silver Stars. I believe my letter home about this battle was the reason he may have thought that.

Mimi Ma, I met her within three hours after I had arrived in Kowloon. Do you believe in Love on first sight? Well that was what happened between her and me. It was nothing like any of my experiences with prostitutes prior to this time. We spent the night we met at the bar she worked out of like a couple of people in love. I was sitting at the bar when she came up to me and asked me if I would like to dance. We danced to that song and many, many more that night. I asked her to spend the night with me where I was staying, the Astor hotel. We closed that bar that night and she and I were together for nearly the rest of my leave. I had spent the bulk of the money I went on R&R with on a silk suit she helped me buy. By my fourth night in Kowloon, I had ran out of most of my money and didn't have enough left to get her out of the bar she worked out of. I told her that I could not spend my time with her as long as she had to prostitute herself while I was there, so I left the bar and went out on my own. Unbeknownst to me, her Mama-san, her boss, had a change of heart, and told her that she could spend the rest of my R&R with me, at no cost to her or me. I think she realized that I was truly in love with Mimi and her with me and let her go. She spent the night looking for me and unfortunately she never found me at places we had gone to prior. She was waiting on me when I returned back to my hotel late that night and we briefly had an argument about my intentions. The fact that I returned to the hotel by myself ended that argument. We spent the rest of my time in Kowloon together and she was with me at the airport when I left that magical place.

The compliments my father gave me on my writing abilities are probably why you are reading this story. He gave me the belief that I was capable of doing this.

CHAPTER 33
OPERATION UNION II

On May 26, 1967 our battalion along with Fox Company of the 2nd Battalion, 5th Marines were lifted out by helicopters to an area that was about 20 miles northwest of Tam Key in the Que Son Valley for some more searching and destroying. This was the start of Operation Union 11. Also accompany us was the 3rd Battalion, 5th Marines and three units of the ARVN Rangers, a pretty good fighting group of the South Vietnamese Army. I always felt better when we went to the field in large numbers. Safety in numbers, I would always say. But the way things were going lately, I knew we would be in heavy combat real soon.

On June 2nd about 12 noon our reinforced battalion came out of a lightly wooded field and stopped at the edge of a dry rice paddy, which was about 100 yards wide to our front and about 200 yards long. Directly across from us was the Vine Hay Village, or I should say part of it, the other half of it was to our left down at the other end of the rice paddy. A small hill that jutted out from the Que Son Mountains separated the two parts of this village. To our direct right was another small hill of about the same height as the other hill separating the village. Within minutes after arriving, our battalion started receiving sniper fire from the left part of this village. Air and artillery were called in to soften up our objective. While this was going on, my squad, which was the squad running point for this movement, which put us on the right side of the on-line movement of the battalion, was told to go up the hill to our right. Once we were up on the hill, we spotted two males who came out of concealment from behind a rice paddy dike and started running across the rice paddy towards the village. The order was given to take them out. These guys must have been doped-up on something, because every time they got hit and went down, they got back up again. This went on till they got almost to the village when finally they went down for the last time. My squad was called back down and we joined the rest of our company who were ordered to advance while firing on line to the part of the village to our direct front. Anything was fair game. We crossed to the village receiving no returning fire. Searching the village only turned-up two very old elders of the village. I found them in one of the bomb shelters this village had. In my search underground, I also found what I'm sure was part of an elaborate tunnel system that connected the two parts of the village and the surrounding area. We didn't have the time to search them completely, so engineers were called in to collapse the tunnels found, to at least prevent any possible use of them from that part of the village.

After our company cleared this part of the village, we went back into the rice paddies and got back on line to move to the other section of this village. We brought the old folks along and I had them walk in front of my squad. I paid particular attention to the path they walked, trying to see if they were trying to avoid any possible booby-traps that they would know about. Just their body language was telling me to be very aware.

From the hill at the other end of the rice paddy an unusually high paddy-dike went from the base of that hill to the other side of the rice paddy, connecting to some higher ground on the other side of it. My point squad was on the right side of our movement to the other part of the village.

When the company was about 50 feet from this dike, the NVA opened fire on us. Unbeknownst to us, the big dike was hollowed-out and filled with NVA soldiers, who were part of the 3rd NVA Regiment. This regiment had set up their base in and around this village. Their defensive positions were impeccable and nearly undetectable until you were right on top of them. When the NVA soldiers initially opened fire on us, they caught more than half of our company wide open with their fire, with nothing to protect them from the barrage the NVA were laying down on them. Most of these Marines were either killed or badly wounded in less than a minute. An outcropping of the same hill protected the rest of the company from direct fire. What was left of the company immediately got up on the hill and destroyed the NVA soldiers in the dike. Fox Company, 2-5 was to our left on the outside of the rice paddy. They too walked into a similar ambush with similar results. Captain James A Graham who was part of Fox Company headquarters section led a group of his staff to give assistance to his beleaguered Company. He died as a result of his heroic actions that day and was posthumously awarded the Congressional Medal of Honor.

From the village behind the dike, we started receiving sniper fire. This guy was good; he was hitting any exposed area, usually the head of the Marine who was trying to locate the position from where he was firing. I had worked my way up to the top of this hill and found some decent cover. Once I figured out his location, I commenced my own fire on him. After nearly an hour and close to firing over a hundred rounds at his position, I figured he had to be in a bunker and I was going to need heavier firepower to take him out of this battle. I had not received my own M-79 that the squad leaders carried in our company, so I passed the word down the hill for the other squad leaders to move up to my position. First one up was Corporal Smith; one of the old salts that secured Chu Lai. He got up with no problems and following him was Corporal Peterson, my fellow point man. Only problem was that Peterson was moving to my position standing up like he never learned anything in the M.C. I wasn't sure why he was coming up in the first place; he wasn't a squad leader prior to this battle, though it's very possible he was made one during this battle. The point is he had what I needed, a M79, but coming up like he did offered a partial silhouette to the damn sniper who hit him in his left upper chest with the round coming out his back followed along with part of his lung, and then falling down right by my position. I think I may have gone a little crazy when this happened. Peterson and I had been running point together prior to this operation and you become real close to that person. After calling for a corpsman, I took his M-79 and both Smith and I fired the M-79's with several direct hits to the sniper's position. Unfortunately, even that was not enough, he was still in action and I was determined to change that. I thought this guy must be in some kind of a reinforced bunker, and the only way I was going to take him out was by going down to where he was and do it.

I was starting down the hill for the village when Corporal Smith told me, "There's no way you're going down that hill." I replied, "You're going to have to shoot me to stop me." Realizing he wasn't going to stop me, he said, "At least take one of your men with you." I said, "No way am I going to take one of these new FNGs with me, he would just get in my way." One of my new guys butted in, saying, "I'll go with you." His name was Lance Corporal Santo; this was his tenth day in Vietnam. There was a fair amount of cover on this side of the hill that we used going down it. I used the M-79 again on some suspected positions while we descended down the hill, mainly individual hooch's that had open apertures facing me. I would fire only one shot at a time and immediately move further down and fire again in an attempt not to give my position away and hopefully make anyone observing me, to think maybe there is a movement coming at them. Once we got down the hill and were at the edge of the village, I decided to move to the right first before I entered the village and try coming up on his flank. I went about 50 feet firing the M-79 along the way twice into the same hooch from different angles. We had about a five-foot embankment that bordered the village for cover as we moved in that direction. We stopped when we came up to an opening leading to the village. After giving the immediate area a visual going over and seeing nothing that would impede our move into the village, we got down on all four's and used some shrubs to conceal our movement along the inside of the embankment to a spot that looked good to me to make our move further into the village. In a low crawl, we moved maybe another thirty yards when I saw the edge of a trench and the head of an NVA shoulder in it. Believe it or not, that dream I mentioned before briefly came back to my mind. I decided to move a bit closer for a better shot. I aimed in on his head and squeezed the trigger. I'm not sure why, maybe the close proximity, but I didn't know if I got him or not, so I started moving towards the trench to find out. That was my first major blunder [or brain fart as some people say] that should have caused my demise. My mistake was I didn't make a checkout of the immediate area first before I made that move. Moving out in a duck walk with my M-16 in my left hand and Peterson's M-79 slung over my right shoulder, I had moved only maybe a foot when I felt this incredible shock go through my body. There was another NVA soldier some 20 feet off to my right in another trench. He fired his AK-47 at me, hitting my right forearm just below my elbow, hitting the bottom edge of my ulna bone, fracturing it lengthwise. The bullet came out of my arm and went into the M-79, went through the round in it, [the propellant part of it, thank God,] and put a bubble on the other side of the M-79. The impact slammed the M-79 into my side, lifting and throwing me up through the air some 15 feet. When this happened, I dropped my M-16. Fortunately, when I landed I was facing the NVA soldier who just shot me. Within seconds I realized where I was shot and that the wound didn't look life threatening. I also saw the M-79 that stayed with me next to my wounded arm. I had no idea that this weapon was now worthless to me. The NVA soldier was sticking his head up from the trench checking out the situation. I could see my M-16 off to the right between him and me, and Santo a bit further to the right. He was frozen in position, so frozen I don't think the NVA soldier realized he was there. I started whispering "Shoot him, shoot him." Santo wasn't firing back. The NVA soldier must have heard me because he looked startled and started looking all around him for the sound. I guess he thought I was dead because he was looking elsewhere. When he was completely turned away from me I picked-up the M-79 with my left hand, aimed in on him and squeezed the trigger. The only thing that happened was the primer of the round had gone off releasing just a trickle of smoke rising up from the breech of the weapon. I wasn't too sure what was going on with the M-79, but I kept it aimed at him, hoping it would fire. When he turned his attention back to me and saw the M-79 aimed at him, I bet he had a shit, because he quickly ducked back down in his trench, As soon as he did, I was up moving for my M-16 nearly the same instant, and yelling at Santo to give me some cover fire, which he did. As I was bending down and reaching for my M-16, I yelled at him again to get the hell out of there and he did. I grabbed the M-16's sling while at the same time holding the sling of the M-79 and got then slung over my left shoulder while running full speed back the way we came into this place. I was running nearly a straight line for the embankment forgetting we came into this place more to my right. As I was coming around this bush, I got the shock of my life when I realized that the NVA had put punji stakes sticking out from the embankment on this side of it. I didn't hesitate a second while running right at it and leaping up and over it, making a flip in the air to land on my feet on the other side. The flip in the air came from my younger years on the diving team at the country club and high school team, the adrenaline to do it from the situation. Even more incredible, when I landed on the other side, my helmet traveled some 5 feet further on and I wondered why. Looking at it, I saw that a bullet had gone through the top of it and wondered why I didn't get hit from the round. That's when I remembered that I had about six letters from Mimi Ma, the girl I met in Kowloon while on R&R, stuffed in between the webbing and the top of it. They probably raised the helmet at least an inch higher on my head; which in turn probably saved my life. I hated to leave it where it was, but it was exposed to possible fire and I had had enough of that already.

 I moved along the embankment until I caught up to Santo who was shaken-up a bit but otherwise OK. I was not too happy with Santo for not firing at the NVA soldier when I first told him to, but kept it to myself for the time being. We managed to get back up on top of the hill to some relative safety. I passed the word down for a radioman to move up to my position while the corpsman worked on my wound. When one came up, I started telling him that that village is full of NVA soldiers and he needed to tell who ever he had to that it would be a good idea to blow the hell out of it. A second later, I was all over Santo, telling him to get his weapon aimed in the direction of that village and to blow away anything moving down in it. A few minutes later my platoon sergeant passed the word up the hill to my position for me to get my ass down to his position. When I got there the sergeant began to chew my ass out but good. Yelling at me, "Who the hell gave you permission to go down into that village? You're an idiot, you're real lucky you're even alive." As I was trying to explain why I did he just told me, "Shut up; where the hell is your helmet and weapon?" "I left them up on top of the hill and I think the M-79 I took with me isn't working anymore and I'm not too sure what I can fire now and my helmet is down in that village." My sergeant was not a happy Marine. He yelled up the hill to pass my weapons on down to his position. When they got to us, he started checking them out. This is when I realized for the first time that the bullet that went through my arm was why the M-79 wasn't working anymore. My sergeant dug out the bullet that was still in the M-79, and gave it to me, saying "You're one lucky Marine; keep that as a little reminder." He found me another helmet and gave me a 45-cal. pistol. Once he had me all squared away, he told me to move over to where the other wounded Marines were gathered. Thinking about how close I just came to getting myself killed was starting to sink in; and for the first time in Vietnam, I was experiencing the true feelings of fear.

The problems for all of us were just beginning. Just before the platoon sergeant told me to move over with the wounded, he got a call over his radio from the command post. He was told that a sizeable NVA force was on its way in a counter attack; coming at us from the same direction we used coming here to this village. He was to gather all the able-bodied Marines he had and bring them back to the command post and to leave the wounded Marines where they were.

There were nine of us wounded; with two of them being so bad off that they each had to be carried by a makeshift stretcher and one able-bodied radioman. We were gathered about 50 feet from the hill on a path by the rice paddy. Not very long after what was left of our company moved out, we started receiving incoming mortar rounds. One of them landed where the platoon sergeant and I were not all that long ago. I was making a lot of promises to God at this point. After the incoming mortar rounds landed, one of our own helicopters made a sweep over us and the damn door gunner fired his M-60 machine gun right down the path we were straddling. I knew if that helicopter came back, we were going to try our best to blow it out of the air. We had bright reflector panels all around us, indicating wounded personnel and still this asshole door gunner opens fire on us. What the hell else are you supposed to do when something like this happens? Thank God that that door gunner missed all of us and didn't return.

As the night was coming on, a full-scale battle was going on. We couldn't see it, but we sure could hear it. From what I've read later on, if it weren't for two companies from the Second Battalion, 5th Marines, that made a dangerous night landing by helicopters in a counter attack, you most likely would not be reading this story.

With the mortars and the wacky door gunner trying to kill us, we decided to move to some large rocks about 50 feet from where we were that were surrounding a well out in the rice paddy. It was decided that we would be safer there and that it would be worth the risk for all of us to get there. We got there with no problems. The rocks afforded some very good cover and protection and before this night was over we were going to need all of it.

Darkness came shortly after we all got to the rocks. In the village I got shot in, there was this hooch on fire. Between the burning hooch and us, we started observing an increasing number of NVA soldiers moving in a column out of the village in the direction of the counter attack against our command post. Inside our rock enclosure we had one M-60 machine-gun, but only about 500 rounds for it. We also had a few M-16s that were in working order.

The problem with these M-16s was that when you were going to fire them, you were never sure if they were going to fire or jam on you. The slightest piece of dirt either on the round going into the chamber or in the chamber itself could cause the casing of the round to fuse to the chamber wall when fired. It is now believed the problem may have been caused from the ball powder used in the rounds, which somehow messed-up the cyclic rate of fire. The original M-16s didn't have an ejector mechanism by the chamber to clear such a jammed round. The only way to clear a round in the M-16s we had at that time was by putting a cleaning rod together and putting it down the barrel to break the fuse and then clear the round. You might as well have been back in the Revolutionary War when you had a single shot musket that had to be reloaded after each shot. This may have worked well in that war but not in this one. A lot of good Marines died with cleaning rods down the barrel of their M-16s.

Over the next hour, we used up all the ammo for the M-60 machine-gun and most of the rounds for the M-16s. We had taken out a lot of the NVA soldiers and all we had left were a couple of 45-cal pistols. With about fifty NVA soldiers making their way towards us we were going to need a lot more help than what the 45s could do for us. I really thought there was no way we were going to get out of this one.

Our radioman finally got direct contact with an F-4 Phantom jet with a Marine pilot at its controls. The burning hooch was the only way we could let him know where we were. We used pop-up flares to let him know where we were in relation to it. That was all the information the pilot needed. This pilot was a very brave and skilled in that not only did he have to be precise where he dropped his napalm canisters and firing his 20mm cannons, he had to immediately pull a near vertical exit out of there or end up crashing his jet into the Que Son Mountains that were directly behind this village. On his first run, he used only the cannons, the next and third run he dropped napalm while firing the cannons, killing an untold number of the NVA soldiers. Between his runs he told our radioman where we could locate what was left of our company and that we needed to clear that area fast because we were about to let loose with everything we had available on that village. We were on our way out when he made his third and last run. I later read about that pilot receiving the "Distinguished Flying Cross" for his action that night. He surely deserved it.

Before we moved out, we decided to split up into two groups, with each group taking one of the Marines on the stretchers. I led our group back the same way we came into this hellhole, back into the rice paddies towards the first village we had cleared earlier that day. The other group went in the direction of the command group. With all the search flares that were being dropped by aircraft and artillery, we had a tricky time of it getting back to our lines, moving only after they went out and it was dark again. About a half hour moving this way, I saw some movement out in front of me. I waited until they were nearly on top of me when I whispered, "Who goes there?" "Is that you Mac?" was the reply and after letting out a long deep breath, I said; "Miller, is that you?" "Yeah-man it's me, they brought me back here to save your sorry butts." "Well I'm sure glad that they could spare you." Miller, who was leading a search patrol looking for us, had come down with malaria a month earlier and was med-evacuated out early on during this operation. He pointed out where in the village I could find what was left of our company. I told him where I thought the other group might be by now and with that said we both moved our groups out again. In 20 minutes or less, we got to the village and what was left of our company. In the first hooch that I went into, I found some of the guys from my platoon and was warmly reunited with them. The mood all of a sudden turned grim when I asked where the rest of my squad was. Fits told me most of them were either dead or badly wounded, except that he thought the new guy Lance Corporal Santo got captured by the NVA and most likely now was a POW.

We didn't have time to give much thought to this fact, because shortly after Fits told me this, all hell started breaking out at the other part of this village. We were using every weapon in our arsenal on the NVA. There were two "Puff the Magic Dragons," AC-47s that flew around the battlefield with each of them firing three 7.62mm Gatling guns with each gun being capable of firing 18,000 rounds a minute. Looked at another way, that's saying in one minute it could put a round into every square foot of a football field. Not only were there "Puffs" working in our behalf, there also was the air and artillery support intermittently working-over the village and nearby areas. The intensity of all this firepower was very frightening and nearly paralyzing. Even sitting down low in the hooch amongst fellow Marines was not comforting enough. I left the hooch, found a furrow in the ground, lay next to it and with my left hand worked on it most of the remaining night to make it deeper. At one point during this entire incoming ordnance, I saw something nearly as big as a Volkswagen Beetle fly nearby through the air. I was praying with all my heart for it to all stop.

As the sun began rising the next morning, most of the heavy incoming ordnance had ceased. Any of the NVA soldiers that could flee the area were long gone, but were easily picked off as they fled across open fields later that morning. Once the sun was up and it felt kind of safe again, I got up and started checking out the nearby area and was taken aback for a moment when I started to see all the carnage caused by all of our firepower. I was having a hard time believing this was the same village we came to yesterday. The other part of this village where I got shot was nearly vaporized now. In and around it nearly 500 mostly dead NVA soldiers were lying about. Among them were a lot of our troops. It was so bad that later that day for the first and only time during that war, a truce was called between the opposing forces so teams could go in and remove their respective casualties. Though I didn't get to witness this, I can imagine it to have been very strange to do so.

The casualties for the 5th Marines from this battle were 71 killed in action with Corporal Smith being one of them who was killed in the ensuing battle that night. There were 139 wounded and two missing, with Corporal Santo later listed as a POW. The other Marine was never listed as a POW or ever found.

    Later that morning, from the top of the first hill I went up at the beginning of this battle, I was med-evacuated back first to Tam Ky where a MASH type unit was set up and my wound was evaluated. It was here that I watched way too many body bags come in. An hour or so later, I was taken by helicopter to a hospital in Da Nang and operated on. I was able to see out of the helicopter on my way to Da Nang and realized that this was the last time I would be in a helicopter flying somewhere in this country and had mixed emotions about that. After I had woken-up after the operation in a ward, one of the first things I asked was about my buddy Peterson. I was trying to find out if he came through there and if he did, what was his condition. The person I was asking said to me, "Why don't you ask him yourself, he's in that bed next to you." I turned around and was looking over at him when he lifted his head up towards me trying to grin and told me to, "Put a sock in it, you "Devil Dog". He was in bad shape, but was going to make it. Two days later, I was on a plane headed for the hospital at the Clark Air Force Base in the Philippines, located near Subic Bay, effectively ending my tour in Vietnam.

CHAPTER 34
DYING DELTA

It wasn't until recently that I became aware of what happened to Delta Co. after I left Vietnam. To be honest with you, I thank God I was shot when I was because my company went on new operations on a regular basis starting right after Union II, on up to and including Operation Swift. Operation Swift was particularly bad for my old company; the casualty list was nearly the same as the list after Union II. The very high number of the dead and wounded from April 5, 1967 to September 15, 1967 earned the company the undesired nickname "Dying Delta."

My regular tour in Vietnam, had I not been shot, would have ended November 3, 1967. I'm not too sure what I would be like today had I survived until that departure date. All I do know is that it was nearly 10 years after that war to where I began to feel somewhat assimilated back again in my own country. It's possible, had I completed all of my tour, to have never been able to find that feeling. War takes a terrible toll one way or another on those who participate in it. For many of the survivors of war, if they're lucky, will realize as I did, that it is much more preferable to resolve a situation by using our brains instead of our fists if at all feasible. I pray that all the world leaders someday come to that realization and stop putting the youth of their respectful countries in harms way. There has to be a better way to resolve problems besides going to war and killing ourselves.

For war only begets more war.

I would like you to know that the 5th Marine Regiment was the most decorated unit that fought in Vietnam. The following is part of a clip from a newspaper dated Oct. 18, 1968: "The President yesterday presented the Presidential Unit Citation to the Fifth Marine Regiment for "extraordinary heroism in action" in Vietnam from April 25 until June 5, 1967

The Regiment was cited for its outstanding performance of duty during Operations UNION and UNION II in the Quang Tin and Quang Nam Provinces of the Republic of Vietnam.

Brigadier General Kenneth J. Houghton, former commanding officer of the Fifth Marines, accepted the award from President Johnson on behalf of the regiment in ceremonies at the White House.

During the period covered by the citation, the Fifth Marines, Reinforced, was assigned the mission of finding and destroying the enemy forces, their supplies and equipment, in the northern areas of I Corps".

I'm not going to give you the whole citation because most of what it has to say can be found in my story, but I'll give you the ending:

> "During the period of Operations UNION and UNION II, the Fifth Marine Regiment inflicted more than three thousand enemy casualties and, according to reports, eliminated the 2nd North Vietnamese Army Division as an effective fighting force for many months.
>
> "By their aggressive fighting spirit, superb tactical skill, steadfastness under fire, consummate professionalism and countless acts of individual heroism," concludes the citation, "the officers and men of the 5th Marine Regiment Reinforce, upheld the highest traditions of the Marine Corps and the United States Naval Service."

The 5th Marines were presented a second PUC for their actions during the 1968 Tet Offensive in the battle for the Citadel that was located in Hue City, Vietnam.

I will always feel proud and honored that I served my duty in Vietnam with the Best of the Best fighting force in the Marine Corps.

CHAPTER 35
GOING HOME

After completing a bit more then seven months of being in country in Vietnam, I began my trip back to the USA that had a few layovers. The medical staff at the hospital in Subic Bay realized that the wound in my arm had become infected and I was transported to Guam to be treated for the infection. The kind of infection I had was quite common, it came from a round that was either pissed on or dipped in shit. Both sides did this, as it was a way we could kill our enemy if the bullet we hit them with didn't do it outright. Unfortunately, this was a fact that "All is fair in Love And War".

I spent the next three and a half weeks in the hospital at Guam. My forearm, when I first got there, had swollen to nearly three times its normal size. During the operation in Da Nang they had opened my arm from my elbow to my wrist to remove bone splinters that had traveled throughout my arm, messing up my muscles but missing all the nerves, tendons, veins and arteries. Upon my arrival and my initial observation, my doctor grabbed my wrist with one hand and the large bandage covering my wound with his other hand, which by now was intertwined with the flesh on my arm and with one movement ripped it from my arm. I was told later that they heard my scream two floors above me. I passed out from the initial pain.

It was at this hospital that I was able to call home for

the first time and let them know of my situation. I could have picked a better time to do that; my parents were in bed after a long night celebrating their 25th wedding anniversary with family and friends. My mother answered the phone and once she realized that it was I calling, she screamed, "John, its Paul!" and handed the phone to my father. My dad got on the phone and like a doctor that he was said, "You've been wounded, haven't you?" I replied, "Good guess, how did you know?" "Figured you had to be because if it was worse this call would be from someone else." I told my father all about how it happened and that the wound was no big deal and once I got rid of the infection in my arm, I should be on my way home.

During this time, I got to experience prescription drugs, pain pills to be more precise. It got to where I could time when the drug would kick in, when a feeling of euphoria would start coming upon me before the ceiling would start to spin. This all happened within the time it took me to smoke a cigarette, ten minutes tops and then I would be somewhere else. It was so nice a way to escape from your present situation that I recognized then that it could very easily become addictive. The skin on my body was going through a transition while I was in this hospital. Really cleaning your body, especially the last couple of months I was in Vietnam, nearly didn't exist for any of us in my company. We had a few times at field showers but you just got off the top layer, while in Guam whole sections of the skin on my body, mostly parts that were exposed, came off in sheets and you could see the ground-in dirt in these sheets.

I was also starting to have problems with the doctor who ripped off the bandage from my arm when I first got here. He liked telling me that he was going to get me back in shape so he could send me back to Vietnam. I didn't care much for this doctor; I felt he could have given me something or done something to my arm to prevent the pain he caused me and made it very clear to him that my time in Vietnam was over. He didn't know it, but one of my father's best friends was Congressman Jimmy Burns, who at the time was the head honcho of the Armed Services Committee; and he was able to prevent that from happening if it came to it, but it turned out it was unnecessary.

Three and a half weeks later, I finally left Guam, with a brief layover in Hawaii so the plane could refuel. While I was there I had another presentation of a Purple Heart from some General getting a photo-op. I was presented this medal at every hospital I had been in so far, making the visit at Hawaii when a general came on the plane to present it, the fourth medal I now had. I was only wounded twice. After crisscrossing the USA, dropping off patients at each stop, we finally got to the hospital at McGuire Air Force Base in New Jersey. It was at this hospital that I got to see my parents for the first time in nearly a year. Somehow, after showing my parents the bullet that went through my arm, it turned up missing. I suspected that my mother kept it that night to throw it away the first chance she got. The next day I was taken by bus to the Philadelphia Naval Hospital [PNH], where I would spend the next six months recuperating.

CHAPTER 36
RECUPERATION

During the six months that I spent in the PNH, life once again was mostly good for me. I got into a routine in the hospital; starting my day off with some physical therapy on my arm, then start my working day in the patients' affairs office, where I would deal mostly with the many amputee patients. The PNH during the Vietnam War was the main receiving hospital for amputees who were in the Navy or Marines from the eastern states. During my time there, we admitted on average about 450 new patients a month; one month I remember it was 487 new patients, making it a real crowded place. Meeting and seeing these men go through that hospital and how they learned how to deal with their own reality that the war caused them, was a learning experience in its own. It was amazing to me, the resiliency of the human sprit and in most cases, the inner strength these patients had to muster-up every day just to be able to function in the world they had to deal with.

For awhile, I used to get any of the girls I could that worked in the hospital to join me and a few of the amputee patients for a night on the town, usually at a bar in South Philadelphia. Believe it or not actually a few marriages came about from my cupid playing. One of the girls became my lover for a time. This was one weird situation; one of the girls and me hit it off, in that we liked dancing together and having a good time. Never during this time did I give this girl any indications that it was anything more than that. In the first place, she was married to a corpsman that was in Vietnam during this time. I wasn't the type to mess around with a married woman, particularly someone whose husband was in Vietnam. Well at the end of six months, I got a 30-day convalescing leave from the hospital, which I will tell you more about in a little bit, but when I came back to the hospital after this leave to be discharged from it, I went into the hospital PX for a few things and ran into this girl who was working in it. When she found out that I had gone on this leave, she actually started yelling at me about it, yelling, "Why didn't you tell me you were going on leave? All this took me aback a bit. I knew her, but as I said before, I wasn't interested in this girl and didn't think I had done anything to give her that idea. Now I was having second thoughts about that decision and asked Cathy if she would like to meet me somewhere when she got off work. She said she would and we did; for the next two months we played house together, sharing an apartment together in South Philadelphia. All was good until my replacement showed-up one day. Cathy knew I would be getting orders for my next duty station soon and apparently had found a replacement for me already. He was a nice enough guy and he and I went down to the corner bar to discuss this bit of an embarrassment. He was having a hard time figuring out what was going on. I was at first also a bit confused, that is, until I figured out what she was up to. After I filled him in on what I thought was going on, I told him to look for two moles she had that only someone who was intimate with her would know about. With that said, looking a bit perturbed, he got up and abruptly left the bar and the bill for the drinks for me to pay. To say the obvious, that was the last time I saw her.

You may remember that I had sent my old girlfriend a "Dear John" or I should say, a "Dear Angel" letter after about six months into my tour in Vietnam, mainly because we didn't agree on much of anything. Well, about a week after I had returned, I gave her a call on the phone. Her mother answered it and was already crying when she answered the phone. After a minute or so talking to her, she finally told me Angel was in the hospital recuperating from a miscarriage. She told me to come by in a few days when Angel would be home. The only reason I wanted to see her was to get back the engagement ring I had given her. I couldn't believe it when I got to her home; she told me that she had met her new husband shortly after she got my last letter and she got pregnant not long after. Her husband was there, but wouldn't come out of the room he was in to meet me; had it been me in his situation, I may have done the same. She gave me the ring and that was the last time I saw her.

A lot was going on in my life once I was at the PNH. The first weeks were like a homecoming of sorts. Just about all my family, relatives and friends showed up during this time and we had some really good times together. One night, when I was in the recreation room, I ran into the first girl I ever kissed other than family or relatives and who I took to the only prom I ever went to. She was a "Candy stripe-Girl"-they got that name I think, because on the uniform they wore were horizontal pink stripes- who volunteered at the PNH. That meeting was kind of awkward. Never saw her again after that meeting. Life for me was getting so good the staff put their foot down and started curtailing my old corner buddies from visiting. My friends were sneaking in to the hospital some booze and we were becoming a little bit too disruptive.

At the end of my fourth day they declared me ambulatory, where at 5:00 PM from that day on I was able to leave the hospital and not have to be back in it till 8:00 AM the next day. Once again, I found myself back in the area of the old corner, this time legally hanging-out at the taverns in the area. I felt quite at home in these bars. Almost all of the locals knew me and were treating me to a lot of free drinks; or I was winning them playing either darts, pool, or pushing a metal-disk on a shuffle-board table after I started getting some more movement in my arm. I seemed to always have had the good hand and eye coordination needed to play any of these games and always did my best trying to excel in any of these games I played. The drawback of all this playing and mostly winning was the excessive amount of booze I was consuming. I was often drunk and started having quite a few fender benders as a result. It got to the point where I wasn't allowed further use of "Old Reliable", the 1964 Ford Falcon Station wagon and for a while had to depend on friends picking me up or using a bike to get around. I discovered I couldn't ride a bike very well when drunk and fell down many times when I tried to make a turn. I also found out that getting drunk seemed to lessen the impact of what that war was doing with my mind. Nearly every night, I was reliving the nightmares of Vietnam in my dreams and often woke up as a result of them. It seemed the more booze I consumed, the less the impact these dreams would have. This was not good and I was becoming more aware of it each day as I went through this cycle.

On one occasion when I was stationed at the naval base, after work, I agreed to meet a fellow Marine at a bar in his neighborhood. This bar was down the road a mile or so from the neighborhood I hung-out in, and was a bar that I was not a regular of. I found the bar and within minutes of going into it, this big twenty something year old bouncer started giving me some unnecessary verbal crap. I now had the full use of my arm again, and being a good armwrestler, soon found my-self in a contest with this bouncer. This guy was a good six-footer who was much bigger than I was. Like I said before, I had been arm-wrestling now for some time and my opponents were always bigger than me.

This guy was rather easy to beat and I even held him to a draw with my left arm. After he paid me the $5.00 I bet him, I challenged him to a game on the shuffleboard table. I was kicking his ass pretty thoroughly in all the games that we had played, and was doing it again, when he started saying or I should say, started yelling some really challenging, personal bull-shit at me and my friend. Well this guy had been one hell of a loudmouth from the get-go, and with his latest tirade, I decided he needed his butt kicked. I challenged him to go outside with me and try kicking my butt. He didn't respond. I walked to the door and told him I'll be waiting for him outside. After five minutes passed and he hadn't come out to fight me, I went back in and yelled-out some pretty nasty crap at him, where he had just about no other choice but to come outside and fight me; finally a few minutes later, he came outside and we went at it. Besides knowing how to box, I was also a good street fighter; which helped me even the playing field against a larger opponent. He wasn't a bad fighter himself, and gave me a decent fight, but he was tiring and I was taking advantage of it. When the fight was broken-up by the two brothers who I knew, who owned the wholesale beer distribution business that was next to the bar, I had by then bloodied him good. This fight happened the same year that the movie [The God Father] came out. After just seeing this movie, I went to a bar called Paul's. This bar, along with the bar I had the fight at, was on about a three mile strip of businesses on or just off Rising-son Avenue. Smigle's was just one block off that avenue about midway along it. Shortly after going into Paul's, the bartender introduced me to this character that looked like he had a role in that same movie. My mistake was mentioning this observation to him. He became highly agitated when I said this, ending up calling me a punk. I briefly told him that I wasn't trying to insult him, and walked away from him and that part of the bar. A few minutes later the bartender called me back to where the two of them were. Again, I told him I wasn't trying to insult him, but that it was good that it didn't turn into something else because my friends at the bar wouldn't like that. I should have giving that statement some more thought before I said it. This time he pulled out a 38 cal. pistol and had it aimed at my chest when he started calling me a fucking punk. I told him "You made your point" turned away from him and started walking to the other end of the tavern, silently praying he wouldn't put a round into my back. He left shortly afterwards. The bartender told me later on that I was very lucky that I didn't get shot by that guy; that he was the personal bodyguard of the mayor of Philadelphia.

It was to be nearly ten years later that I was finally able to break free from this cycle of almost daily drunkenness. Ironically, it was getting drunk with John, a fellow Vietnam Vet and raising hell with him that ended this cycle. The next morning after waking up in the car he slept in that night, John went back into that same bar, had one drink, said he didn't feel well, went back to his car and died. When I learned about this, it made me begin to truly examine my own lifestyle. From that time then, till now, I have stopped drinking liquor of any kind. If I were to be pulled over by the police, I would pass a breathalyzer-test, because when I go out now, I drink only beer, at a pace of less than one beer-per-hour, which would and does keep me under the limit of .08. It was also the passing by his gravesite everyday that got me into saying prayers for others on a regular basis. I don't travel out that way much anymore, so I pray for him and others I think of as I walk from my car in the morning to start work at the post office. For some of the people that I prayed for, it seems to have worked. Praise God.

It was during this same time period after I stopped drinking liquor that I began reading about Don Juan, a Shaman among the Yaqui Indians, where in the third book in the series, Don Juan describes to Carlos Castaneda what he thought constituted a true warrior. That definition changed me over the years into what I think I am now. But I'm getting ahead of myself now and later on I'll go more into this matter.

Back in the PNH, I thought that the physical therapy authorized by my doctor was inadequate, and I finally convinced one old female therapist to go beyond what the doctor had ordered. When I first got the cast off my arm, I had minuscule movement in it. To change that, I convinced this therapist to tape to my hand, at first, a one-pound weight and I would let gravity work on stretching my arm out. Months later, when the doctor authorized weight therapy; I was up to a thirty-pound barbell. I was trying to extend my stay at PNH, so when it came for me to be examined by my doctor and he was measuring my progress, I would always stretch my arm only partially. I kind of doubted that this doctor was falling for any of my acting; as for one thing my arm was getting noticeably larger from all the physical therapy. I liked this doctor; he was a congenial young man who had a great bedside manner. The first time I got to meet him was shortly after I got admitted to the PNH. After his initial examination, after the cast was removed, he told me straight out, "I don't think you will ever get back full use of your arm, you had a lot of muscle damage to your arm. It will be very hard to make them work again." I took this as a challenge and told him straight out, "Before I leave this hospital my arm and muscles are going to work good enough to beat you in an arm-wrestling match, Sir, I'm willing to bet you $30.00 I will." This doctor was no more than five years older than me, but was a good six-foot tall, nearing 190 pounds. Now he was the one being challenged. He smiled, and then he chuckled and said, "You got it, Marine."

With the challenge accepted, I did everything in my power and imagination to be sure I could back up my end. At the hospital I convinced the therapist, nearly every other day, to increase the weight she would tape to my hand. At home, I would get any of my brothers or sisters to open-hand box with me or throw softball with me- anything I thought would force me to stretch my arm out further. It was working; almost everyday I could see improvement in my strength and flexibility. I had pain from all this, but I refused any painkillers other than aspirin. I didn't want to numb my pain, because I used it as a barometer of just what I truly could or could not do with my arm.

About a month after I was admitted to the PNH, a friend of mine and of the other guys from the corner was admitted. He also was a Marine and would end up spending just over a year recuperating in that hospital. His name was Joe Doyle and before getting hit in the thighbone from a 50 cal. machine-gun bullet, was every bit of a jock and participated in most outdoor activities. The round that hit him blew out nearly three inches of his thighbone, but not all of it. A few slivers of bone remained and over the next year he would go from being in a near full body cast to months of having his leg in traction, then back to the body cast, allowing the bone to grow back. I watched Joe, a very gung-ho Marine arrive at this hospital, then over time he evolved into one of the biggest critics of that war during the short time I knew him there. His hatred of the war may have been the catalyst that got him through all the pain and mental anguish he felt while confined to that bed. None of this prevented or impeded his recovery. Four years later, I met him again at the same place I first met him, at his family home that they had on the Machamity Creek, outside of Philadelphia. He was doing the same thing he was doing when I first met him, ice-skating and doing it just as well. I was happy for him. It was on that same ice that I again had a brush with death, and later that same year, doing the same thing over water. In both incidents, I was using a tree swing, a rope that was hung from trees. You used them to swing over the water. Up on the Machamity Creek that winter, while visiting my friend Joe Doyle, I used the rope to swing out onto the ice and then let go and slide quite away on the ice. I had done this many times, but on one swing, I wasn't lined up right for a good slide, so I held on to the rope for another try; when the rope and my body became nearly horizontal with the ice, the rope broke and I came down onto the ice hard, hitting the back of my head hard enough to knock me out for nearly 45 minutes. I woke-up in a hospital. Other than having a pretty big bump on the back of my head, I felt fine and was discharged. That summer, some friends and I went to some creek in N.J. I was doing the same thing except over water you let go of the rope when you were horizontal, to do flips before hitting the water. On one try, I never even got to the water; there were two different jump spots in the tree to start your swing out over the water. I had been using the 30-foot jump when I decided to try the higher 40 foot one; the only problem was that I had too much slack in the rope when I jumped from it. Having too much slack caused the rope to snap out of my hands when I and the rope were near parallel with the ground directly below the jump spot. Lady luck or maybe my Guardian Angel had something to do with it, but when I landed, it was on my right side with my arm tight against my body, absorbing most of the impact. The air was knocked-out of me, but other than that, I was OK. Had I landed in roots like a young teenage girl did that same day, that put her in a hospital, I could have ended up a lot worst than I did. About a half hour later I went off the 40-foot jump again, this time I got to the water.

CHAPTER 37
DISCHARGED

Near the end of six months in the PNH, my doctor showed up one morning to again checkout the progress I was having with my arm. After looking at it he finally said, "Well my friend, I'm afraid what you are showing me tells me we have done all we could for you and I'll be starting discharge proceedings today." I replied, "Come on doc, I still think I can get some more flexibility out of this arm, don't you?" "I'm sure you can and probably already have, I believe you've been fudging it a bit with me, my friend, don't you?" "You knew all the time, didn't you doc?" "Your therapist has been filling me in on your progress from the beginning." "I just didn't want to lose that bet we made when I first got here. You do remember that bet, sir, don't you?" "Yes I do, but before we do any arm-wrestling, I want to reexamine your arm, this time show me what you can really do with your arm." "No need to check me out again, sir. As you can see, I have regained total flexibility and a hell of a lot more muscles; maybe enough of them now to beat you in an arm-wrestling match. I have been arm-wrestling for a while now and may have an advantage over you. I won't blame you if you decide to decline, you can just give me the $30.00 and I'll be on my way" "Not so fast my friend, let's check your arm and if looks as good as you're saying then we will see about giving it a try." Once he was done with the exam and agreed with me that I now was completely healed he said,

"OK, we will arm-wrestle, one time and that's it, for thirty dollars, winner takes all." I think the doc gave it his best, but as I told him I been working out my arm in matches with some pretty big people and winning. The doctor was in good shape, but my arm was the stronger one that day. Doc was a good sport, not only did he give me the $30.00 bucks, he told me that I could have a thirty-day convalescing leave back at my home before I had to report back to duty. I didn't expect the leave and was very thankful for his generosity.

CHAPTER 38
SILVER STAR

It's possible that he may have felt like I had it coming to me for what I did to get the Silver Star Medal, which was presented to me by the Commandant of the Marine Corps, General Wallace M Green on September 27, 1967 in the PNH. It was great; it was truly my 15 minutes of fame. The entire major TV news stations and the local newspapers and radio stations had people covering this presentation and I was interviewed by most of them. All of my family and friends were at the presentation. It's pretty cool when you get to see yourself on the front page of a major newspaper, or listen to yourself being interviewed on TV or radio. For at least a week after, I didn't have to buy any of my drinks when I went to the bars, for the good people of Philadelphia wouldn't let me.

Whenever I got the blues, I would read the citation that came with the medal, and doing so, would get me right out of my doldrums. I would like you to know how it went.

In the name of the President of the United States, the Commanding General, Fleet Marine Force, Pacific takes pleasure in presenting the Silver Star Medal to Lance Corporal Paul A McNally, United States Marine Corps. For service as set forth in the following Citation:

"For conspicuous gallantry and intrepidity in action while serving as a Fire Team Leader with the Second

Platoon, Company D, First Battalion, Fifth Marines, First Marine Division in connection with operations against the enemy in the Republic of Vietnam on May 12, 1967. During Operation Union, while advancing with the platoon's leading elements, Lance Corporal McNally observed twenty North Vietnamese soldiers to his direct front. After the fire teams immediately deployed and engaged the enemy with intense and accurate fire, it soon became evident that the enemy force was a small element of an estimated two reinforced battalions of North Vietnamese Regulars. As the full force of the enemy's firepower was brought to bear against the Marines, Lance Corporal McNally, armed only with an automatic rifle, skillfully maneuvered to a flanking position. Unhesitatingly exposing himself to enemy fire, he delivered a deadly volume of fire into the North Vietnamese positions until he had expended all his ammunition. As a result of his accurate and intense fire, four of the enemies were killed, numerous casualties were inflicted and his unit was able to gain fire superiority. Maneuvering through heavy enemy small arms fire, Lance Corporal McNally returned to friendly lines where he replenished his ammunition supply from wounded comrades and commenced a second trip toward the enemy when he was wounded by mortar fragments.

Due to the overwhelming number of the enemy and numerous Marine casualties, it became necessary for his unit to withdraw to a covered position.

Disregarding his injuries and refusing medical aid, Lance Corporal McNally steadfastly remained in position to provide rear security and courageously maintained an accurate, well-aimed volume of fire at the enemy.

Only after receiving assurance that his unit was in a covered position did he withdraw to receive medical attention. By his courage, determined fighting spirit and selfless devotion to duty, Lance Corporal McNally upheld the highest traditions of the Marine Corps and of the United States Naval Service."

Like I said earlier, just reading this citation usually got rid of any blues I might be having. You've got to appreciate the guy who wrote this citation. As I said earlier, I was just doing what I thought I should be doing.

* Official U.S. Marine Corps photograph
1ˢᵗ Photo – Silver Star Presentation

* Official U.S. Marine Corps photograph
2ⁿᵈ Photo – Silver Star Presentation

CHAPTER 39
REALITY

You would think that by now since I was out of Vietnam that I would probably be safer with a lot better chance of not getting myself killed. It just wasn't going to be that way. Beginning when I was going home for thirty days of convalescing leave, it turned out that I would end up using 29.5 days of that leave to recuperate from three cracked ribs I received the day I started the leave. I was lucky that was all I got that day. This misfortune came about starting the night before my leave was to begin. The first factor involved came from my watching Steve McQueen in the just released movie called "The Great Escape", where he escapes on a motorcycle from a German concentration camp. The other factor was my buying a 90cc Ducat Motor Bike the same night from a corpsman that was shipping out for Vietnam.

It was a nice morning that day when I left the hospital while traveling west up Broad Street on my new motorbike. Traffic was pretty heavy and I was behind this big truck when all of a sudden this truck slams on his breaks. We were traveling about 35-40 miles per hour when this happened. I was too close to the truck to stop in time, so not even thinking about it, I got down low on the bike and managed to steer to the right side of the truck and got under the high lift on the rear of the truck without hitting it, coming out and getting between the truck and the cars in the next lane and somehow managing to get it under control from there. I made the rest of the trip without incident. The real problem came later that day when I decided if Steve McQueen could get a motorcycle up and over a fence then I could do it too. I didn't have a fence to go over, but I had a good imagination. Our house had a large front yard, and if I came down the street in front of my house, into my neighbor's driveway, and on into my front yard, I could hit the ramp I set up with enough speed that I could go over this imaginary fence with no problem, landing on the down slope of the yard. After doing this stunt four times, I set the ramp a bit steeper and hit it a bit faster on my fifth run. This time instead of going up and out, I went straight up, with me going up with it and coming down on my side into the handlebars, cracking three ribs. I immediately got up and started running around in a circle trying to get some air back into my lungs. After what I thought was like a lifetime, I managed to start breathing again. I knew I had messed up my ribs but was not sure how bad until my father came home that night and checked me out. He did what he could for this kind of injury, wrapped me up in Ace Bandages around my ribs. The true pain didn't hit me till the next day when I tried to get up from my bed in the morning. For the following weeks, I needed assistance getting in or out of my bed; I truly never felt pain like it. It wasn't until near the end of my thirty-day leave that I became able to function somewhat like I did before this accident.

When my leave was up I reported back to the hospital to be discharged. That was the same day I ran into Cathy as you may recall. My next three months were spent at the Philadelphia Naval Base, while waiting on orders for my next permanent duty station. For the most part, my time there was a sham as far as I was concerned. It took me two years to make Corporal and when I got to this base I was told to do the same shit work that I was doing before I became a NCO [Non-Commissioned Officer]. I was told, "all the lower ranks were in Vietnam, and guys of your rank are all we got to keep this place up." I went on a couple of burial details during this time and hated doing it, in that just the act of burying Marines at that time in my life was too close to my past reality and I just wasn't ready for that kind of detail. Enough said.

CHAPTER 40
LAST DUTY STATION

I finally got orders to report to the base at Quantico [Virginia] where my new job was to train new Marine Officer Candidates. When I first got there, I was on a medical profile, or light duty, another gift from my doctor, which meant I actually never did this job for a couple of reasons; the first and in my mind the most realistic one was: "What I knew to survive was something I felt that I couldn't teach to these people. It was either by the grace of God or just pure luck that I survived that war, and I'm going to teach them that. I just didn't think I could. The other reason was that although I did my job when asked and did it as well as I could, I was just not ready to be a fighting Marine again or try training officer candidates, especially since I was for the first time thinking we should not even be or ever should have been in that war. I was learning there was much more going on that I had no idea of when I went to Vietnam, such as the way our leaders of this country were micro-managing that war from Washington, D.C., and not letting the military truly do their jobs in Vietnam. A lot of our troops were getting killed directly or indirectly because of that fact and this was beginning to piss me off. Frankly, I believe the same thing is happening right now with the present administration. The similarities of the two wars looked at from a strategic and political view is like witnessing history repeating itself all over again. Hopefully, this country in the future will learn from history and not continue on the same path followed by several U.S. Presidents during the Vietnam War.

I hate to say it, but we should let the "Surge" in Iraq have the time to work. It is possible that it might work, in that if we can suppress the bad guys long enough to where the population can feel safe enough with the people of their own country truly protecting them, once we rid an area of the bad guys; then it might work. We had the chance to do the same thing in Vietnam after the 1968 Tet offensive- the V.C. and the NVA got their butts kicked during their attempt to overrun most bases then. Had we followed up and taken the offensive to them then, that war might have had a different ending. The same can be said about our present wars. Give this some deep thought.

By the time I got to Quantico, all I wanted to do was finish up my time in the M.C., hopefully learning something, you could use as a civilian, other than killing people, which is all I had learned up to that time. A month or so after I got there, the company I was assigned to was to have a CG [Commanding General] inspection. If you had a gripe or needed to talk to the General about something you could request to speak to him during the time of the inspection. I got to speak with him and pretty much told him what I told you. Surprisingly, he agreed with me and soon after I was given a new assignment. I started working in the photo lab we had on the base. I learned how to develop film and process it. After a couple months of doing that, I was assigned to work in the M.C. film archives. This was a good job and I got to check out some great old war film. I was looking for film that had the most famous Marine of all time, "Chesty" Puller in them. He fought in a lot of different wars and there was a fair amount of film with him in them. A movie was being made about him and they wanted all this film to see if they could use it somehow. Just this year, the Postal Service put out a stamp with his portrait on it.

One day while I was working, this great General showed up in our building and shook hands with all the Marines there. When I met him I felt incredible humility and honor that I was actually shaking this great man's hand. He pointed out and mentioned my Silver Star and Purple Heart ribbons on my uniform and told me, "Good job, Corporal" and moved on to the next Marine in line. It may be hard to believe, but I got to meet the general a second time. It was about a month later, after I had been given a new job. My new job was one that most Marines would be proud having. I was now part of the elite guards who worked in securing the original Marine Corps Museum located on the Quantico base. Part of the job was explaining the different exhibits on display. Over time, I became comfortable and competent in this position. When we were on duty, we were in Dress Blues that were issued and cleaned by the M.C. One day while I was on duty, General "Chesty" Puller and a small entourage came into the museum. When he came up to me he actually remembered meeting me before and said to me, "You sure get around on this base, don't you corporal? This man alone probably saw and participated in more wars and combat than all but a few Americans and if he had his way, he would have been the General that ran my war too. There are several good books written about this man and it's worth the time to read them.

CHAPTER 41
PARTY TIME

My life during the year I spent at Quantico was rather wild, in that I was "living on the edge", as they say. When I wasn't working, I was drinking hard and partying hard. I had two different places I could go to off base and live this way. In the town just out of the gates, my buddies and I rented a small house and we also had an apartment in Arlington, Virginia. It was at a party in Arlington that I nearly bled to death. Some girls we knew were having the party and all was fine until I saw a guy I didn't know trying to make a move on one of the girls, being very insistent. When I realized that she didn't want any part of this guy, I moved over to them and mentioned that this girl was married to a Marine friend of mine who was in Vietnam at the time and it sounds like Patty here is trying to tell you to back off. Considering that I was a few sheets to the wind when all this happened, I never saw the sucker-punch he hit me with that knocked me down, but not out. As I was getting up from the ground, saying, "You're going to wish that you never did that", the son of a bitch threw a tumbler-glass into my face, cutting deeply from above my left eye down my cheek nearly to my lip, cutting the tear duct in my eye and my nasal artery in half. To say I was bleeding profusely would be a big understatement. I was told later that when they got me in the house, I covered a couch and a nearby rug with my blood.

My Marine buddies were in a conundrum; you see we were what could be considered AWOL. At the time, a lot of unrest was starting to break out in D.C. related to the race riots happening in other parts of the country and we were on stand-by in case we were needed to go there. Sergeants or above could leave the base as long as they left a phone number where they could be reached. A good part of my platoon had made plans on going to this party, including a few sergeants, problem solved. The conundrum was that if I went to a hospital I would be considered AWOL, but if they didn't send me I most likely would bleed to death. I was taken to a hospital and when they realized I was an active duty Marine they transferred me to Bethesda Naval Hospital. Once again, I was lucky in that there was one of the best plastic surgeons in the country and he did his magic on my face and tear duct. Talk about luck, the operation he performed on the tear duct was one that only three years prior to that time didn't even exist and this doctor was one of only a handful of doctors who knew the procedure. He used 129 very close stitches to sew me up and today you would not even know my face was split open, if I didn't point it out to you. I was in the hospital recuperating close to three and a half weeks.

During my stay there, a couple of things happened that are worth mentioning. The third day I was there, the guy that hit me came in to visit. At that time, I was confined to my bed, had a catheter stuck up my penis and my face was swollen, black and blue and looked like shit, about the same way I was feeling. When he came up to my bed, I had no idea who he was and asked him what he wanted. That's when he apologized for throwing the glass in my face. I couldn't believe this was the guy and told him I didn't want his apology, all I want from you is your name and address. He wrote it down on a piece of paper and gave it to me. Then I told him to get the hell out of my sight. A few days later, an officer from the legal department came in to talk with me and at first I had no idea why. First thing he said to me was "I guess you know that you were AWOL when you got your face messed up and that you may be required to pay the medical bill for the surgery done on you." I told him I was not aware of that. He went on asking me if I planned to sue the person who did this to me. I told him I hadn't given it any thought, but I know who did it to me. He told me that they knew who it was as well, and that he was also a Marine who was recently released from active duty. Then he told me if I let the M.C. sue him instead of me then I wouldn't be charged for being AWOL and that I would receive some kind of disability when I got out of the M.C. for the scars on my face. All of what he said to me sounded good and told him I'll go along with it. I signed a few papers and he was gone. Never found out why the M.C. let me off the hook on this incident, or why they wanted to be the one suing. I got a 10% disability rating for my scars when I was discharged. That 10% added with the 20% I got for my arm scars made a total of 30% and at that percentage rate I was able to use all the benefits offered in the Disability Act, along with the GI bill that was offered to all servicemen. I took advantage of these benefits and for ten years following my discharge, I was in school either learning the trades of carpentry and auto mechanics, or getting an AA degree during the rest of the time. Believe me, all that I learned has made my life better in what kind of money I have made and the kind of jobs I've been eligible for; and during those ten years when I was in school, I hate to admit it, but at that time in my life, it beat working for a living.

    A few days after I got back to Quantico I went to the rifle range to get back into an intramural rifle club I belonged to. I was curious if my tear duct would change my sight when firing a weapon. It didn't and on this particular day I was shooting up a storm, good enough that a Colonel who showed up at the range picked me and one other guy and told us to go to the armory and get sniper weapons and zero them in. We were told that we would be on call when we go to D.C. as the battalion snipers. After I went to the range and zeroed in the weapon, I was given an able target to aim on, at 1000 yards. There was no scope on the weapon. I was laying in the prone position with the matched conditioned M-14 sniper-rifle supported by sandbags looking through the custom sites; all that was clear to me was a target that looked no bigger than head of a pin. To my surprise, out of ten custom produced bullets I was given to fire, I put three of them in the 5-V, dead center; five of them in the black, which was a circle with a 20 inch diameter, with the other two rounds hitting within an inch of the black.

While I was in the hospital recuperating, riots started to break out in the black section of D.C. The Army was called in to stop them, but after two weeks they were getting nowhere doing so. So what do you do? Call in the Marines.

I was having some mixed feelings about the possibility of having to use a sniper weapon on an American citizen; hell, I was having a hard time dealing with the fact that I killed enemy soldiers. But I figured if we were called up to use the weapons, it would be for a very good reason. As it turned out, I never had to use it and because I was a designated sniper, I didn't have to stand the many hours of guard duty the rest of the Marines did. Most of the time, I just rode around with the cops and they stayed away from any confrontations they could; I was very happy about that. In less then a week, the riots stopped and we returned to Quantico.

Unfortunately, upon our return, about thirty black Marines went on a rampage on and just outside the base, killing three people and severely beating up a bunch more. Two of my black friends and me were at the NCO club drinking and playing pool together when I had to go to the head [restroom]. When I was in there doing my thing, the lights went out. We had heard about this rampage and I thought that it could be them who put the lights out. Immediately, I started making my way out of the head by keeping my back to a wall that was a partition between the entrance and the toilets. Somehow I managed to get to the other side of the partition without being discovered and was nearly out of the restroom. I started running the last ten feet when I got whacked on the back of my head, causing me to come airborne. In that same moment, I used this momentum to make a single flip in the air, landing on my feet just outside the entrance, turned around and pushed the button on my push-button knife, exposing the blade. I was very pissed off and challenged any of them to come out and try having a piece of me. None of them did and then I recognized one of them. I had gone through boot camp with this guy and told him we will meet again, turned, and left. When I got back into the club, I told these friends of mine what just happened. They suggested that we get out of there now and get back to the barracks. On our way, all of a sudden there they were in front of us, looking for me. My two friends told me to stay where I was while they went and talked with these guys. I'm not sure what my friends said to them, but whatever it was, it was enough because they let me go. All of them eventually went to trial and were given just punishment for their actions that night.

CHAPTER 42
POTOMAC RIVER INCIDENT

Finally, there was the time when six Marines drowned in the Potomac River and I was part of the search party sent out to find their bodies. These Marines were all part of a physical fitness club and on this particular day; they were in a crew boat out on the river when they somehow flipped it over. Since it was mid-winter and the water was very cold, these men were dead in a very short period of time from hypothermia. A couple of miles down the river, we found clothing that we thought might be from one of them and we needed to call in to the base and tell them about this discovery. Only problem was that the radio we had was with part of our group that was up on this bluff above us. We were unable to get their attention and had one of two choices: we could walk about a half mile back the way we came to a spot that was easy going up on the bluff, or someone could climb up the bluff right where we were. The top of the bluff was at least 100 feet or more from the base of it by the river where we were and the first part of this climb was nearly vertical for 40 feet or more and was all rock. After the rock, it wasn't as steep the remainder of the way and consisted of packed dirt, a few exposed rocks and a bit of small tree growth here and there. I thought I could climb up it without too much trouble and volunteered to do so. All went well till I got to the last couple of feet from the top where there was an overhang. As I was trying to get over the overhang, I grabbed hold of a root from a tree and was pulling myself over the overhang, when the root broke off in my hand and down I went, nearly to the vertical rocks. I was only able to stop when I managed to grab one of the small trees just above the drop off. Had I gone over it, I most likely would have gotten really messed up if not killed outright. I was scraped up a bit, but more pissed-off than anything else and went right back up, this time getting on top of the bluff, where I found a couple of Marines sleeping. After I gave them a good chewing-out, I found the radioman and he called in the information. The base told us to rendezvous at the clearing that was just before this bluff to be flown back to the base by helicopter. I decided that I was going back down the same way I got up this bluff and head to our destination with my group. A couple of Huey helicopters came in to take us out of there and all was well until the rear tail rotor blade shorted out on the Huey that I was on. Luckily, the pilot of this craft was a Vietnam Vet and was able to control the descending helicopter into a marsh next to the river without incident. It's my personal belief that the men who flew the helicopters in Vietnam were some of the very best and bravest of all who fought in that war.

CHAPTER 43
END OF MY TOUR

Somehow, I managed to finish my four-year tour of active duty in the U.S. Marine Corps alive and in one piece. Though I was a bit damaged physically and not completely well mentally, I was much better than what I was when I first got out of Vietnam. I thank the M.C. for that because they could have discharged me with a medical discharge when I got discharged from the PNH, but didn't. They kept me in which in turn allowed me over the next fifteen months to release a lot of anger and frustration amongst my fellow Marines who were the only people around that could understand where I was coming from and did, up to a point, put up with it. I thank them for that.

About four years after I was discharged, I began wishing that I had stayed in the M.C. If the M.C. had made me a sergeant before my active duty was up, I most likely would had extended my enlistment for at least a couple of years. I guess how I was thinking back then may have been the reason I was never made a sergeant.

My thinking at that time had turned sour on the M.C., which seemed to be in the mode of eliminating what they considered dead wood. Some Vietnam vets that I had become good friends with were treated very unfairly by the powers that were controlling the M.C. then. They were both thrown out of the M.C., with both given Bad Conduct Discharges. What they should have received was some psychiatric treatment for the PTSD that they were both suffering from, as were most of the guys I knew, including me, who saw combat. In the M.C., and I suppose in most of the services, very rarely back then would something like PTSD even be recognized and if it was, probably nothing would have been done about it. If you were not up and delivering their way, it was just as easy to get rid of you by charging you with something, with often setting-up some of these veterans for failure. It was something I was having a hard time accepting, something that was turning me away from the very thing that I loved, The United States Marine Corps. Just recently, I learned from reading the paper that the Army has discharged over 42,000 of its troops. Most of these troops were veterans who served either in Iraq or Afghanistan. They were discharged at "the Army's discretion", where the Army claims they were not able to function because of a mental disability or malfunction they had prior to joining. Hogwash, most of these people had experienced war and they are suffering from PTSD, and most are not getting the kind of treatment they deserve and need. Hopefully, now that this has been brought before Congress, maybe something will be done to correct this travesty.

CHAPTER 44
CIVILIAN AGAIN

By the time my four years in the M.C. was up, I truly felt we were in the wrong war and that the US should pull out from there. What I see today with the war in Iraq and Afghanistan is not much different from what I was seeing going on in Vietnam: this country imposing our brand of culture in the guise of democracy on ancient cultures that will not change their ways and never will, at least, not by force.

If I had been discharged from the M.C. after I was discharged from the PNH out into civilian life, I would have more than likely ended up on the wrong side of the law or worse.

Within the first year out of the M.C., I received two letters from the CIA offering me a job as an office clerk. Back then; I couldn't see myself being a clerk in some bureaucracy, working in a government institution. Years later, I realized that that's where you probably started working in the CIA, to possibly becoming an operative later on in your "Career". The gut feeling I had back then told me I didn't have what they were looking for, someone who could kill on orders, if that was their reason for wanting me in the first place. Living that kind of life was just not for me anymore. I never responded to their offer. Believe it or not, that same year, I even got several offers to become a mercenary. Again for the same reason, I didn't respond to their offers.

As it was, Olivia, I still had my problems dealing with everyday life. If it weren't for a wonderful lady that I met three weeks after I was discharged from the M.C., my life still might have gone in the wrong direction.

CHAPTER 45
WONDERFUL MARY

Mary and I met at a dance club that had the first electric dance floors in Philadelphia. When I first asked her to dance, I knew I had to get to know her beyond that night and did my best to make that happen. We did a lot of dancing together and as the night was coming to an end, I asked her for her phone number, which she gave me. It was to be three weeks and many phone calls later that she finally agreed to go out with me. That first date turned into many, many more over the next two years. It was during this time that Mary's love and advice to me started the ball rolling in the right direction. I don't think there was a thing that I wouldn't have done for her, including getting my drinking problem under control for starters. This lady was a class act; she worked as the executive secretary for the Captain of the Philadelphia Naval Base and had a way about her that you just wanted to please her anyway you could.

When I was first discharged, I had the opportunity to take off and do nothing but collect unemployment checks for six months. I felt I had at least that much coming to me, considering my last four years. After the six months were up, I had a succession of short-lived jobs over the next two years.

One of the guys I knew from Smigle's Corner knew a foreman who could get me a job working in a metal shop where they fabricated fireboxes for commercial buildings. During the six months that I worked there, I learned a lot about the business and liked working there. My job came to and end when I was moving a bunch of stainless steel sleeves I had welded together and piled up on a skid. As I was moving them, they shifted and were beginning to fall. To prevent this from happening, I reached up trying to steady them. This was the wrong thing to do, a sharp corner of one sleeve cut deeply into my right wrist, nearly severing the tendons and veins in it. I collected workers compensation for about three months. My next job was with one of the major Philadelphia newspaper companies. The job title was assistant district manager, when in reality it was no more than a branch captain for paper routes. The routes were in a tough blue-collar neighborhood and the kids working for me were a rough group of about thirty teenagers. On my first day working in this job, this group was giving me no respect at all. To change that, I asked them, "Who is the best fighter amongst you all?" They unanimously said it was this kid who was about six feet tall. I asked him if he knew how to box. When he said he could, I asked him if he would like to try going a few rounds with me. As I expected, he said sure. I got the boxing gloves that I kept in my car and we started boxing. I more or less gave all watching this fight and the kid I was fighting a demonstration in the art of boxing. From that day on, all my kids worked hard for me. This job came to and end when my boss found out that I knew that he was skimming money from all the branches under his control. When I became aware that he was doing this, I mentioned to him of my suspicions; a week later my boss fired me, giving me some crap why I was fired. The kids working for me weren't happy about my departure and let me know this when they trashed his car in a major way. A week later, I started working for the Good Humor Co. as a stand in. Anytime they needed an extra body because someone called in sick, which was often, I would deliver their route, which could be in any part of Philadelphia and its suburbs or parts of New Jersey. Most of these routes were in run down, poor tough neighborhoods. I had some dangerous days while I was delivering ice cream in these areas. One of them happened in a section of Germantown, Philadelphia when a teenager who I just sold an ice cream bar to on the last block all of a sudden showed up at my window saying he wanted another one because he dropped the one he had. He didn't have anymore money and I told him "no money, no ice cream." When I turned to go back to my seat to move on, this kid jumped through the window from where I sold my products. By the time I turned around, this kid had a knife at my throat saying he wanted another ice cream bar. As soon as I gave him one, he leaped out the window and was gone. I stood there for at least a few minutes in a bit of shock. I was trying to rationalize the fact that not all that long ago, I just survived a war only to come back home nearly getting myself killed selling ice cream of all things. Now pissed off, I drove back to the office and almost quit, only to get talked into staying on with the promise of no more dangerous areas to work in. A week later, while delivering a route in Trenton, N.J. again I was very lucky, in that I didn't get killed. As soon as I started delivering this route I had the feeling that this was not going to be a good day. On the first block of this route, which was in a federal housing project, a young, street savvy, good-looking black girl convinced me to let her ride with me and to do the selling of the ice cream. She convinced me that I would be glad I did. She knew the regular guy that delivered this route and that he wouldn't deliver there if she were not there to help him. She was quite a character; within minutes she was all set up to do my job and was very knowledgeable of how to do it. After riding with me for over an hour and doing a great job, she told me that she had to leave, and suggested that I should do the same. I should have listened to her. When she left, I decided to finish up one more section in the project. As soon as I went into it I saw a local gang checking me out. I saw them breaking up and heading off in different directions, arousing my gut feeling which was telling me something was up and that it most likely wasn't good. When I made the turn onto the next street, I saw part of this gang coming up behind my truck and others coming out from alleyways. I knew that their attentions were not to buy my ice cream. Deciding that I best get my butt out of there, I hit the pedal to the metal. The next thing I knew, my truck was being hit with rocks with the gang converging closer in on my truck. Looking through my side rear view mirror, I saw one of them trying to get into my truck through the side window. When I turned around and saw that he was getting in my truck, I got up from the drivers seat, while the truck was in motion and kicked him hard in his face, causing him to fall from the truck. Somehow, I was able to escape from that project. That was my last day working for that company. The last job I had before I started using the GI Bill to go to school was about a three month stint selling floor tiles at a department store.

CHAPTER 46
WOODSTOCK

One day Mary gave me a list of items that she wanted me to gather before telling me that all this stuff was for the trip we were going to make to the original Woodstock concert. She was with me one day when I was in the old neighborhood seeing some of the guys from old Smigel's Corner. One of the guys mentioned the Woodstock concert that was coming up and after talking about it, we all agreed that it would be a good one to go to. It was a week later that she told me we were going to it and that she had already gotten the tickets for it and all I had to do was fill out that list. But even before that concert, there was a one-day concert at the Atlantic City racetrack that we went to. We were nearly right in front of the stage when Janis Joplin was playing and we were both amazed at her performance. This concert was the prelude to what the Woodstock concert was going to be like: lots of love, nakedness and good vibes. One of the things on the list that Mary gave me was to get a detailed map of the Woodstock area, which I did and because of it, we were able to avoid most of the very heavy traffic that made its way to that concert. We were able to take back roads into Woodstock and park her Volkswagen Bug in a field and set up camp less than a quarter of a mile from the concert itself and had no traffic problems getting there. Using this same advice, we went to the Watkins Glen concert after Woodstock and were able to park less than a half block from where we set up and had a bird's eye view of that concert.

The contrast between the Woodstock and Watkins Glen concerts was like night and day. Though it rained at both concerts, most of the people at Woodstock turned all that rain into a good time, whereas at Watkins Glen, it just exacerbated the many problems already happening. It turned out that Mary and I had a fulfilling good time at both of them, mainly from the appreciative people with whom we shared the surplus of food we had at the Woodstock concert, to the good feelings we ourselves got from helping a couple who were having very bad reactions to some bad LSD that was sold at the Watkins Glen concert.

Do you want to hear some real irony? The main things that still stand out about those concerts in my mind was, at Woodstock, when I drove Mary's Volkswagen Beetle into a hundred yard square field of mud, where I joined at least thirty other Beetles. It was just amazing, like almost being part of a big play, a Broadway play, as we seemed to be doing some kind of choreography while spinning our "Bugs" around in the mud. Where at Watkins Glen, the most remembered moment happened when they set fire to the line of overflowing portable toilets that ran back-to-back for over a hundred yards.

Throughout the relationship I had with Mary, it seemed her main goal was to make a better person of me, mainly by encouraging me to start using the GI Bill to further my education, which near the end of our relationship I started using. Our relationship came to an end around the same time I first used the GI Bill when I started going to school at Lincoln Prep in downtown Philadelphia to take some necessary courses of new material and to take some remedial classes to be able to get into college. It was around this time that Mary's dad died and when I went to the funeral, I was to find out that Mary was engaged to a lawyer to get married. Apparently, Mary was dating this guy when I first met her, which might have been the reason she was reluctant to date me for the first time. I now think that once she got to know me and about my combat experience, she may have felt that it was her patriotic duty to date me, since it was her that I wanted to get to know better. Whatever the reason, I thank her for the wonderful time I spent with her and her great advice she gave to me; without it, I know my life wouldn't have gone the positive direction that it has.

There were other people who had a hand in helping me reintegrate back into civilian life and one person in particular I would like to thank is my Uncle Jimmy along with his wife Anne and their children, you all helped a lot, I thank you.

CHAPTER 47
LINCOLN PREP

Mary was two years older than me and interestingly, I think she knew when I started going to this school that I would be meeting a lot of people closer to my age and whose interests were closer to my own. By now because of her, I was a far cry better person than I was just a couple years ago and was eager to find my place in this society. If she had thought that this would be the case, then she was correct.

At Lincoln Prep a whole new world was opening up for me. Instead of hanging out with what was still available at the old corner, I found myself spending much more time with my new friends. During my time at this school, I met some people who also lived in Cheltenham. This couple, who were Jewish, became the first friends I had with anyone of that faith. Bonnie and Stew were easygoing folks who seemed to have a lot in common with my own desires and beliefs at that time. Because of that and that these people truly made me feel good being around them, caused us to remain friends for many more years after we graduated from Lincoln Prep.

CHAPTER 48
CALIFORNIA HERE I COME

Not long after I finished up at Lincoln Prep, I got an invitation from my brother Mike who was living in Redondo Beach, California at that time, to come out and join him; soon after I started making plans to do just that. With a little research, I learned about a company that would deliver your car anywhere in North America and I became a driver of one of their cars to California. I now had a new 350 Honda CB motorcycle, which I didn't want to try driving across country, but needed to have with me in California. I solved that problem by dismantling the Honda to where I could get it into the back seat of the car I was driving. The night before I was to start my trip, my younger brother Tom asked me if I would take a friend of a friend of his with me. When Tom told me that this friend was a very beautiful girl from France, my resistance to this idea mellowed somewhat. He didn't bother telling me that this girl could not speak or understand English other than a few phrases. Unfortunately, this also was my situation when it came to the French language. It was when I met her that all of that didn't seem to matter. I believe she had the same feeling I had when we first met and that was this was going to be one hell of a good trip. Language aside, we became very intimate the first night and throughout the time we spent together on this trip, Vive la France!

CHAPTER 49
LEARNING THE LEATHER & CARPENTRY TRADES

What can I say about California; for me it was a fresh breath of air. For starters, the people I met were so much more liberated and at ease with each other than the people I knew back in Philadelphia. It was a place where I had no problem being accepted, even if I was a Vietnam Vet. I ended up working for a friend of my brother who was part owner of a company that made custom-handmade leather products, such as belts, wallets and handbags. The working conditions couldn't have been better. The people I worked with were the surfers, hanggliders, skateboarders and motorcycle daredevils who loved what they were doing at work as much as they did loving and enjoying life. They were very good at doing it right in all that they did. I learned most of what could be learned in this operation and after five months in this job, I became one of the designers of what we tooled into the different leather products we sold. This was the time of the flower-power generation and I came up with a simple design of flowers coming off stems that I put on the full length of a belt, then I painted the flowers with a paint made for such products. My boss immediately liked the idea and told me to make ten more like it to show to the sales people. They sold like nothing they sold before and made a hell of a lot of money with my design. I now felt I could do this as a business of my own and decided to go back to Philadelphia and start my own company. For two years after I got back to Philadelphia, I ran a business out of the basement of my parents' home. I employed my sister Sue and four of her friends part-time in this business and cleared nearly thirty thousand dollars the second year, not bad money back in 1973. If I had gotten the contract that I was soliciting with Gimbals department stores, I might still have been in this business. The contract would be the deciding factor whether to invest or not in heavy equipment to streamline the production of my products. No contract was made and shortly afterwards I ended the business.

After a couple of months of free loading and with my parents prodding, I decided to use my disability factor to go back to school to learn how to become a carpenter. I spent a year at the Darrel School of Trades, located in downtown Philadelphia, learning this trade and became quite proficient in all the aspects of the trade. It was at this school that I first saw the sign declaring, "A brain is a terrible thing to waste" and took it to heart. The knowledge I learned there has come in handy on many occasions since.

When I first started this school, I became friends with several of the students and before long was invited to live in what I guess would be described as a commune. In reality, we were just a group of people living under the same roof of a home that was once a beautiful mansion over a hundred years past. Termites also shared the same home with us and were the reason we lived there cheaply. In the basement, one of the main floor joists or beams that were once 4x12 inch solid pieces of wood was so eaten-out by the termites that I could punch my fist right through it. One day when they were swarming, the door that opened up to go down the basement fell off the wall because the wood the hinges were screwed into was now gone, as would the house itself would soon be. It was condemned and less than a year later was torn down.

CHAPTER 50
JANET

About a month before we were given eviction notices, I got to meet another fine lady named Janet who was going to Penn State University to become a teacher and was in Philadelphia doing her teaching internship. I was in O'Malley's, a favorite watering hole for young professionals in Jenkintown Township, near Philadelphia. I was sitting at the bar by myself for a good hour and she was just a couple of seats away talking with some of her colleagues this whole time. Out of nowhere, she starts a conversation with me, which, to make this story short, led eventually into a relationship over the next year. Much like Mary, it seemed her goal was to get me to better myself. When her internship ended, she convinced me to move back to her home which was in Benton, Pennsylvania, a small town located in the foothills of the Pocono Mountains. I fell in love with the area the first time I went there.

At first, I lived in a nearby town called Bloomsburg with a cook who worked in the hotel named the same as the town. Olivia, if you ever find yourself in that town, especially if it's a Sunday, I recommend you try the Sunday brunch at the Bloomsburg's hotel. Picture in your mind a five-foot wide fifty-foot long table with foods from all over the world displayed on both sides of that table. Take my word for it, the food displayed was some of the best found anywhere; for this pleasure it was only two dollars for all you could eat. To say the least, I became a regular every Sunday while I lived there and even a few times after I had moved to Harvey's Lake, it was that good.

CHAPTER 51
STARTING COLLEGE

Did some maintenance and constructions work in that town and sold a lot of belts to make ends meet. Eventually, Janet convinced me to go to a branch campus of Penn State University that was near Harvey's Lake, which was about a ten-mile ride further west of Benton and with Wilkes-Barre- Scranton about ten miles further to the west of the lake. The day I went to that campus to find out if I could enroll, I was very glad that I did. First off, the school itself was in just one building, which happened to be an incredible mansion. After a tour of this beautiful mansion and its classrooms that were rooms that told their own story with incredible woodwork and painted murals in most of them, I thought I would be a fool if I didn't give this place a chance. I might add that the original owner of the mansion was a coal baron of some local coalmines. He donated the mansion to Penn State when the coal ran out. The only provisions to be accepted in this school were that I would be on probation the first semester and would have to attain at least a 2.0 grade point average to continue. I put my mind, heart and soul into that semester and ended up with a 2.8. I might have been able to better that grade point, but I got very involved with the Vets' Club on this campus and for a good reason: MONEY. The GI Bill I started college with was the same GI Bill the Vets that came out of World War II had. It may have been good enough then but with inflation, it just wasn't enough for us, the Vietnam Generation. Too bad they didn't give grades for extracurricular activities. For nearly the next two years I spent many, many hours involving myself in changing that GI Bill. By the time I went to the main campus of Penn State the following year, we had organized every Vet Group on every campus east of the Mississippi River and planned a trip to Washington, D.C. when a newer version of the GI Bill was expected to pass but to be vetoed for the fifth time by President Ford. When that day came, Vets numbering over 50,000 descended on the capitol and had our representative's talk with every elected official ear that we could talk to. The new GI Bill was overwhelmingly passed, minus a lot of "Pork"; and this time, President Ford didn't veto it and signed it into effect. It has since then been changed several times and been given new names, but remains a fair GI Bill of Rights.

About midway through my first semester at the branch campus, Janet was stricken with Crohn's Disease, which nearly took her life. She spent over a half year in the hospital and during this time there, her personality and beliefs changed dramatically. Not long after being discharged from the hospital, she ended our relationship. Janet by now knew that I would be transferring to the main campus of Penn State University in the fall and didn't want to have a long-distance relationship with me. She knew that a whole new world would be opening up for me when I got there and wanted me to take full advantage of it with no strings holding me from it. Janet now had a teaching job in her town and had no intention of doing anything other than that; and because she now was faced with a lifetime of medical problems from her Crohn's Disease, she just thought it would be best if we went our own separate ways. Reluctantly, I agreed with her and just before I left the area, we met once more to say our goodbyes and to wish each other the best of luck, good health and happiness for our futures.

CHAPTER 52
MAIN CAMPUS

Janet was right when she told me that I would find a whole new world when I got to the main campus of Penn State University. The campus and the number of people on it were huge. At any given time, thousands of students could be found going to or coming from classes. It also was a dog-eat-dog world; you were just a number in this vast system of education. It boiled down to the amount of time you spent learning what was going on in each class you took that determined if you were to continue in your education or not. This was the way it was for me and unfortunately the semester that I should have spent doing just that was also the time the GI Bill vote came up and I was just spending way too much time working with the Vet group on this campus on getting all of us a new GI Bill.

CHAPTER 53
DEBBIE

The Vets on this campus were mostly Vietnam era, though there was a scattering of Korean and Second World War Vets also, but it was the Vets that lived in the Vets house on that campus that were the catalyst that organized all the other campuses to go to D.C. when that vote came up. If you had been to that house back then, you probably would have had a hard time believing the people living there were able to do that. If you ever saw the movie "Animal House", then you would have a picture of what this house was like at times. We sure did party hard on many occasions that year. It was at one of the parties that I met Debbie, who was a senior in the school of Nursing studying to become a Registered Nurse. We dated the rest of that semester and had a great time together.

CHAPTER 54
GAINESVILLE FLORIDA

I knew my grades suffered because of all my extra-curricular activities, but I didn't expect to flunk out; unfortunately I did. I had an offer from my brother Mike to move down to Gainesville, Florida. Mike had moved there two years earlier and I had made a visit there over the past Christmas break and liked just about everything I saw and experienced. I hated ending the relationship I had with Debbie, but I didn't see any other way of dealing with it. She wanted me to stay, find a job till she graduated and figure out then what to do. I just had this desire to move to Gainesville and its warm climate more than I wanted to stick around there with the very cold winter we were having. Debbie and I stayed in touch with each other after I left and the following year she moved down to Gainesville for a job at the Veterans Administration Hospital in town. I had worked with a plumbing company shortly after I got to Gainesville; mostly digging ditches or other manual labor they needed for about a half-year at minimum wages, which after that summer convinced me to go back to school. Back in 1976, as it was in most parts of the country, jobs were hard to come by and I learned that I had no choice other than humbling myself in just about everything I was used to if I wanted to stay in Gainesville. Amongst all the things I fitted into my 1968 Mustang Coupe for my trip to Gainesville, were all my tools to work in either the construction or the leather trade; but like I said, the jobs were few as were the people who were looking for leather products, and I most likely got the labor job with the plumbing company only because I had a car that could get us to our job site that was an hour and a half south in Inverness, Fl.

CHAPTER 55
THE BUTLER FAMILY

When I first moved Gainesville, Fl. I was living in a tent my first three weeks here, since my brother Mike didn't have enough room in his small mobile trailer. Mike was living on part of the 66 acres that the Butler family own. The extended Butler family, a very innovative, close-knit family had been living on that land for a very long time, which over the years the family carved out an existence that over time, has prospered. They owned the fledgling plumbing company that I got to work for and I worked hard for them because I appreciated what they had accomplished in their lives. Most of the Butler family, I believe, learned most of what they knew right there on their property from each other. It was truly living with "RED NECKS" on that property, mind you, I was learning that that wasn't necessarily a bad thing, it was just a hell of a lot different from what I was used to. Some of my best friends are good old boys whom I met in those early years that proudly refer to themselves as pure RED NECKS. The Butler's also had on their property a bunch of old mobile home trailers, which they rented out. After my third week living in a small pup tent, I used my first paycheck from the Butler Plumbing Co. to rent one of their nasty trailers. Overtime, I was able to make the different ones I lived in somewhat better, but the trailers were so old that it was a constant battle just keeping any of them habitable; but they still beat living in a tent.

It was during this time that my brother Mike gave me a book to read. It was the first book of this series of books on the same subject, written by Carlos Castaneda, which dealt with supernatural powers of the Shamans, or as some believe, the Sorcerers of the Yaqui Indians. By the time I finished the third book, I had come to realize that regardless of what they were called, they were warriors first and in this vein the sorcerer explained that whatever they did, it was done impeccably, including using your mind to prevent using your fist to solve a dispute. Somehow the information I got out of those books was the impetus that started a long but steady change in how I viewed just what a warrior was and on just what my role as a warrior was or should be. To me it all boiled down to this; "If I could use my brain instead of using my fist, do it". Believe it or not, this one thought has changed my life an untold amount for the better. After I took that belief completely to heart, nearly everything that has gone on in my life was improved. And the funny thing about adopting this theory is my life has become so much more enjoyable since I went this way and often wondered why I didn't figure this out sooner. An example of this was in the ditches I was digging back then. My boss told me he never saw such well cut ditches as the ones I started digging all of a sudden soon after I read the third book. It got me a raise and a chance to learn other aspects of that trade.

CHAPTER 56
SANTA FE COMMUNITY COLLEGE

That fall, I started back to school with a whole new outlook while going to Santa Fe Community College, a great little school in Gainesville, though now it's not so little. It reminded me of the first time I started going to school at Penn State, small classes, and teachers that knew you by your name and gave a damn if you were absorbing what they were trying to teach you. I did well there and went on to get an AA degree towards Journalism, which later on was enough to get me a job I could only dream about and that was the DVOP job working with vets at the employment service; more about that job later.

It was that winter when I moved in with Debbie. The trailer that I was living in was in such deplorable condition, one that had no heat, where on one long cold spell with temperatures below freezing for over three days, the water in my toilet froze into a solid block of ice; conditions bad enough that I finally relented and moved in with Debbie, which is what she wanted ever since she moved to Gainesville. I liked Debbie from the first time I met her and always enjoyed her friendship a great deal, but I believe the girl was in love with me and wanted me as a husband, something that I wasn't giving any kind of consideration to at the time. We lived together nearly a year and at the end of it she convinced me to move back with her to Pittsburgh.

CHAPTER 57
PITTSBURGH

In the late fall of 1978, Debbie and I moved back to Pittsburgh and got an apartment together. Debbie worked as an RN at the Pittsburgh Hospital and I started looking for jobs, which were very hard to come by at that time in that city. All of the steel mills and mines were shutting down and unemployment was over 20% in that area and if you weren't from around there, your chances was all that much more dismal in finding a job. It got so bad that I was on food stamps and welfare and was very depressed with my situation. To make things even worse, the winter we had that year was the coldest and snowiest winter in the last thirty-seven years for that city. I have a picture of my car that was in a lot across the street from our apartment. The entire photograph is of white snow with a bulge in it and my car was the cause of the bulge as it sat there under the snow till the spring.

By the time spring had arrived, I had already made up my mind that living with Debbie in Pittsburgh had to come to an end. It seemed all I could think about was how much I was missing Gainesville and made plans to return there as soon as I got my car in shape to make the trip. When I told Debbie of my plans, she told me she had already figured that out and understood my situation and wanted us to depart on a good note. We spent the last two days and nights enjoying ourselves together in ways we never had before and that made it all that much harder when I left. As it turned out, we got to spend another whole week together. No more than just a few miles out of Pittsburgh, heading for Philadelphia, my car started overheating and I had it towed on back to an auto repair shop down the street from Debbie's apartment. Debbie was overjoyed with my car's problems and for the next week she treated me even better than she did before I first told her I was leaving and all of the things we did were on her, since I had only enough cash to make the trip back south. We enjoyed nearly everything we did together first class and I know it wasn't cheap doing these things, but Debbie wanted it that way and who would say no this kind of enjoyment.

CHAPTER 58
BACK TO GAINESVILLE

I know I made the right decision coming back to Gainesville when on the first day back, I found a job taking care of a few horses on a farm east of town near Melrose. I could live for free in one of the rooms of the home of my new boss, a young woman and sole owner of a horse-riding instruction business that she ran from the farm.

This worked out well because I was able to do the job with the horses and go back to Santa Fe Community College, this time to get a degree in basic auto mechanics. I really liked this place because it had a virgin cypress swamp that was about one square block in size. My love of the discoveries found in nature was fulfilled every time I ventured into it. I used to daydream of having my living quarters built on stilts right in the center of the swamp; I often thought it would also be a great place to do some writing in.

Unfortunately, all good things come to an end. It seems I wasn't paying any attention to my boss and landlord, in that I never tried making a move on her. Not too sure why I didn't; she was an attractive young woman.

Guess the chemistry just wasn't there, but whatever the reason, one night she started banging on the door to my room and when I opened it she started screaming at me some gibberish along the lines about the fact that I hadn't taken any liberties with her and it was driving her nuts and that I would have to go. I packed up and moved out to where my brother Mike was living the next day and stayed there till I got messed up again.

CHAPTER 59
CONSTANT REMINDER

While I was living at my brother's place, I continued with the auto mechanics course and even used my latest car, [a1973 Ford Pinto], as one of the cars we worked on. The Mustang I had was stolen and I never saw it again. On the last day before the Christmas break, we assembled my car back together, but it was a bit out of tune. I thought the distributor was not seated right and pulled into a parking lot not far from my brother's place to try and adjust it. It was the wrong thing to do and to make a long story short, I nearly had the thumb on my left hand completely ripped off when it went between the fan belt and the wheel rotating the alternator. It was held to my hand by just a few strands of skin. Once again, I had major trauma happen to me, but was lucky enough that two medics just happened to be in the hardware store that was next to where this accident happened. By the time the ambulance arrived, the medics had already cleaned and bandaged my hand and thumb. I was even luckier to have one of the best in the field of microsurgery work on me. In this case, the doctor who put me back together was considered at the time to be the best in the field of micro-hand surgery. Again this was a new procedure and this doctor just happened to be here in Gainesville to teach this procedure. He did a great job reattaching my thumb and all the things connecting with it. It may be a half-inch shorter but other than that it feels and functions just as well as it did before the trauma happened to it.

I would like to make note that this accident to my thumb happened in the very same parking place that John, the Vietnam Vet I mention earlier in this story [that I got drunk and raised a little hell with] had parked that night and who had died in his car the next morning. Well, I now have a constant reminder not only of John, but also something to remind me to never drink liquor again. God works in mysterious ways.

CHAPTER 60
DVOP

About six months later, after recuperating at my parents' home, I came back to Gainesville and went to the Florida State Employment Office to find a job. My time spent at the same kind of office in Pittsburgh had taught me the ropes of this kind of business and I thought I knew what to expect when I went there: a lot of runaround and very few job opportunities. As it turned out, I ended up with a job working in that very same office. The Vet-rep I talked to that day was a college-educated Jew who was about my age; he was the man in charge of that office's section. Every state employment office in the country had a veteran's section, where a vet looking for a job could deal with a fellow vet when he went there. Larry Bayer was his name and he served four years in the Air Force, but never went to Vietnam. After he looked over my resume, he then looked at my DD-214, which was my military history on one page. I watched this man go from a gruff, matter-of-fact kind of person to an animated happy-go-lucky type of guy. It turned out that I had just the bare qualifications needed to fill a job they had an opening for; which was having at least a two-year college degree, be at least 30% disabled and have at least three months in a job that dealt with communicating with people; the sales job that I had in the department store filled the latter and I put in for the job when it was offered.

On August 22, 1979, I became a DVOP [Disabled Veteran Outreach Programmer] and started my dream job of working with my mind, helping veterans get themselves back into the working world and dealing with employers to offer these vets the jobs they needed. In most cases, I was able to help most of the vets I dealt with and found much satisfaction in doing that. Larry and I became great friends during the four years I worked along with him in that office and we stayed in touch with each other for years after I left for the post office. I'll be forever grateful to Larry for offering me that job and arranging the hour a day to work on my memoir the last year working with him.

CHAPTER 61
USPS

About six months into the first year that I was in this job, the USPS notified us of the test that was going to be offered to fill positions for city mail carriers and clerks. These were very coveted jobs to have in Gainesville at that time, mainly because of the salary and the health and retirement benefits they offered. The job at the employment office working for the State had all of this too, but on a much smaller scale. I now had a new girlfriend that I thought I could end up being married to; and thinking about the future, I took the test to get into the USPS

Three and a half years later, I started working as a mailman [or a city letter carrier as the post office refers to us] and come January 7th, 2009 I'll have worked 25 years for the USPS. With the four years that I spent in the Marine Corps, I'll have 29 years of government service counting towards retirement. If my health holds out, I'll most likely work with the USPS till I'm 66 years of age in a job that I take much pride in performing and love doing. I have at last learned to be civil and a servant, in the sense that everyday I am useful to other people.

Well, Olivia, I think I have answered most of your questions and maybe a few you didn't ask and the ones left I'll answer briefly. Presently, I'm a member of several veterans' organizations but I'm not an active member in any, mainly because at the present, I just don't have the time. Once I do retire, I plan to become much more active. The same could be said about going to reunions. As a member of the 1st Marine Corps Association, there have been several reunions that I would have liked to have attended, but again, just haven't had the time. This summer, I'm going to make the time and will attend my first reunion with the First Marine Division Association. Someday I hope to hold a reunion for the members of my old unit, Delta, 1 /5, 1st Marine Division. Though I'm not too sure how many of them survived their tours or whether the ones that did would want to get together and hash over the times we spent in Vietnam. I'm still going to try to get together with the ones who do. Time will tell.

From this story you may conclude that I may have been some kind of Don Juan when I was a young man. I guess between my natural curiosity and testosterone surging through my body, I may have seemed like that and to some extent, I may have been. In actuality, it was mostly learning experiences for me while searching for the perfect mate. The sex I had with prostitutes was just that: sex, no love or passion was involved, though Mimi Ma was an exception. As for the other women in my life, there was love and passion, but not enough of it for me to want them as a wife and in most cases for them to want me as a husband. I actually never contemplated getting married to anyone except Angel, and that was for a very brief time.

CHAPTER 62
KAREN – MY LIFE PARTNER

I would like to tell you how I did find my best prospect yet. I met Karen when I was thirty-one years old. I was leaving a party, the annual Great Sagittarian Party. Jay, a good friend of my brother Mike, threw this party for nineteen years in a row. The final party happened the same year Jay got married. The party was outdoors in the countryside and as I was walking down a dirt trail to get to my car, I heard a voice from the shadows saying, "What's the rush, good-looking?" I knew right away that this person must be near-sighted. I stopped and walked over to two women who were sitting on a log and said, "Who's asking?" Karen replied, "I am, you're not leaving, are you?" "Well, I was on my way home, but I could be talked into staying a bit longer if you would like that." Karen said she would and for the next month following that party, she and I spent a lot of time together getting to know each other.

I was living with Debbie at that time and that's when she convinced me to move to Pittsburgh. I guess I moved with Debbie to see if there was the possible chance that our relationship could be more than it was. It didn't take long for me to realize that it wasn't going to happen for us. The thought of spending the rest of my life in that part of the country and her world just didn't appeal to me and I realized that it never would. Knowing that Debbie wouldn't be happy anywhere else made it clear to me that it would never work for us, so I came back to Gainesville.

A year later, I ran into Karen at the annual spring arts festival held downtown, but we only talked briefly with each other at that time. About a year later after that meeting, I stopped by a friend's house and just when I was about to ring the doorbell, the door opened and standing there was Karen who was just leaving. We talked for a bit and I got her phone number. We started dating again and not too long after we were living together. The following year we got married and soon thereafter we were graced with a baby boy we named Shawn. He turned 26 years old August 22, 2008, coincidently, it was August 22, 1979 when I started working as a DVOP and on the same date in 1983, I was informed that I had been accepted to work for the post office. It is also the day I finished up this story in 2008. I hope this is a good omen and that my son will also succeed in life, for he seems destined to follow in my footprints when I was his age. From very early childhood Shawn exhibited the same penchant for fighting I did when I was growing up. And I spent a lot of my time training him to do just that. He is talking about getting into this new craze of extreme fighting. When I first got home from Vietnam, my younger brother Jim expressed the desire to become a fighter. I taught him as much as I could in the skill of boxing, along with telling him that is a good thing to know how to box, but even better yet, how to use your brain to get what you want. I apparently even at that time realized this, but it took me to actually read the same thing in another book before it finally registered. My brother Jim took that advice to the extreme. Not only did he become a very good boxer, he went on and got his Masters Degree. For the past 22 years, Jim has been the head boxing-coach of the United States Naval Academy. Jim is also an International Boxing Referee, and was the only American out of 500 referees worldwide to be chosen as one of the 35 who refereed at the 2008 China Summer Olympics. I'm hoping my own son sees the light and will follow a similar path.

This past February 12th Karen and I celebrated our 26 anniversary. Given the divorce rate in the USA, this is quite an accomplishment. It confirms my belief that any situation can be changed for the better with time, love, and a lot of patience and understanding.

Gainesville is a fairly small city with a population of around 200,000 permanent citizens. When I first moved here in 1976 the population was under 100,000. I was living out in the countryside west of Gainesville. The rural areas around the place I stayed back then have today become gated communities. Back then most of the new construction going on started during the expansion west of Gainesville that still is going on, though today you will find new construction going on in all parts of the city and all directions around it.

This area of Florida has activities to offer for nearly anyone living here. Name just about anything one could participate outdoors in and you can find it here, even ice-skating, sorry no snow skiing. Downtown Gainesville has become quite exciting in the last decade. With the colleges and additional 70,000 thousand students going to them, it can become pretty nuts at times, particularly after winning two national championships in the same year. The University of Florida's football and basketball teams won national championships in the same year, and for the basketball team the second year in a row winning the championship, a feat that only this school has accomplished.

In a just published book, surveying 500 communities and rating them on fourteen different factors – health care, traffic, cost of living, cultural opportunities, outdoor activities etc. – Gainesville came out # 1 as the best place to live in the USA.

One of the people who had a hand in this development was Ed Clark, who became my first good friend in Gainesville. It was at his house that I ran into Karen again. For a while he was married to Alice, the friend of Karen's who was with her that night at the Sagittarian party. Running into Karen at Ed's house was one of the main reasons I started dating her again. I felt for some reason that our relationship was meant to be.

Ed bought the original Purple Porpoise, a bar/ pool hall/ dart room that he renamed Eddie C's. In 1976, I met him while playing pool there. He was playing a game of darts with Mike Harold, who turned out to be one of the finest persons I ever met, God bless his departed soul. I grew up with an American dartboard in our basement, but they were playing completely different games on an English dartboard. They explained the differences. Since the act of throwing the dart is the same, I was able to impress them with my skill; to such an extent that Ed invited me to join his team in the new dart league. Thirty years later, I still throw darts on occasion, but most of my spare time is spent now in the pool league or playing in pool tournaments. At first, I used to play either darts or pool four or five nights a week, but I've had to cut it down to one night a week because I'm spending more time with another love, writing. My wife and I decided to downsize and moved out further from the city and because we did this just when the housing bubble burst, we are facing foreclosure on our old home of 21 years. Now with the rising gas prices, I now only play in the Monday night pool leagues.

When I was younger, I acted and played the games more like a hustler would; and made a lot more money than I lost. Now I see myself as a teacher of the game of pool, mostly 8-ball, sometimes 9-ball. Throughout the years I have watched several generations of young people come through that bar, and associating with them has been a learning experience for me. I have learned that in life, what you get out of it is equal to what you give back of yourself to it. Many times I have seen in these young people glimpses of what I was like at their age. I hope my influence will better their lives. While I am teaching the strategies of playing league 8-ball, I find ways of passing along any wisdom that I may have accumulated, as well as the lessons of life I have learned; using the pool table as my blackboard. I guess you could conclude from this letter that my time spent in the Marine Corps has had a significant effect on my life and that it still does even today. There is an old saying in the M.C., "Once a Marine always a Marine." Whenever I come across a fellow Marine, regardless when active, we greet each other saying Semper Fi. It reaffirms a bond that made us brothers or sisters in the best fighting force in the United States. This alone puts us at ease with each other, unlike what we would be with most other people we would meet for the first time. Semper Fi and its meaning to me has carried me through many obstacles and trying times. It has given me the belief that nearly everything worth having or doing can be made possible. Putting up with the almost "Boot Camp" situation I went through the first year I started working in the USPS can also be credited to this belief. My beliefs are so much of me today that my body language apparently displays it. From how I now see the way people react to me tells me that it is a good thing and I'm still working to make it better.

 Olivia, as your mother can tell you, I was nearly the opposite in personality and reaction when I was first discharged from the M.C. I drank too much, still got into fights, some with fellow Vietnam vets, mainly from complete ignorance or false beliefs. I was living a life without direction or goals; today, having these two beliefs have made my life worth living for and, if necessary, fighting and dying for.

 I'll always be grateful to the women in my life who were able to see that there was a better person in me and eventually were able to bring it out. Goethe was right in praising the Eternal Feminine, as a source of inspiration.

CHAPTER 63
SUMMARIZATION

It's time, Olivia, to summarize my life as I look back on it now: Though my father was a medical doctor, I failed in my youth to follow his good example. Instead, I hung out with a street-corner gang, kept getting into academic and disciplinary trouble at several schools, dropped out of high school. To give some sort of meaning to my life, I joined the Marine Corps. To my credit, I aspired to be part of the best. My pugnacious spirit stood me in good stead there. In Vietnam, I was wounded twice and was awarded the coveted Silver Star for gallantry in action. This was the high point of my life. I had done something that put me on the front page of the Philadelphia newspapers and appearances on the major TV news stations, and made my parents proud.

Back in the USA for operations and a lengthy rehabilitation, I had a hard time readjusting to civilian life: a series of dead-end jobs, including ditch digging, a series of dead-end romances, a problem with alcohol, a lack of purpose. The nadir of my life came when I was subsisting on food stamps and collecting welfare and living in a dilapidated trailer where the toilet froze.

I now savor the inspirational message from Buddha: The fine lotus flower rises from the deepest muck. Thanks to the influence of two women, I made the effort to better myself. I got into college. Then I held down a worthwhile job with the state of Florida helping vets get back into this world.

Under the influence of my bride-to-be, I began a long-term career in the USPS. I have settled down after a turbulent life. I have a wife, a son, a steady job; and we are living in a warm and pleasant college town.

Throughout my odyssey of adventures and misadventures, my detours and blind alleys on the road from high-school dropout to solid citizen, was it the Hand of God that protected me in war and peace and guided me along the upward path and became my Redeemer?

Sincerely, SEMPER FIDELIS,
Paul A. McNally

INDEX

Afghanistan, Pgs. 1, 196, 197
Albert, Pg. 54
Alice, Pg. 240
Almeria, Spain, Pg. 49
Angel, Pgs. 27, 43, 48, 49, 51, 52, 88, 164, 165
Arlington, Va., Pg. 187
Army of the republic of Vietnam– [ARVN], Pg. 141
Aunt Feenie, Pgs. 110, 113, 137
Aunt's: Alice, Pgs. 87, 137
Aunt Anne, Pg. 205
Aunt Mary, Pg. 137
Barcelona, Spain, Pgs. 48, 49
Benton, Pa., Pg. 213
Bethesda, Naval Hospital, Pg. 188

Big John Liberty, Pgs. 65, 66, 67, 69, 71, 73, 79, 114
Big John [Smigel's corner], Pg. 23
Bill [Smigel's corner], Pgs. 15, 16, 17
Billy Broken Arm, Pg. 5
Bill Muldoney, Pgs. 28, 39, 40, 41
Bloomsburg, Pa., Pg. 213

Bonnie and Stew, Pg. 207
Brig. Gen. Houghton, Pg. 156
Bronze Star, Pgs. 135, 138
Buddy Farington, Pg. 110
Butch [Smigel's corner], Pgs. 19, 20, 21
Butler Family, Pgs. 223, 224

California, Pgs. 51, 52, 53, 209, 211
Camp Geiger, N.C., Pgs. 38, 39
Camp Lejeune, N.C., Pgs. 39, 41, 43, 45, 51
Camp Pendleton, Calf., Pgs. 51, 52, 53, 133
Capt. [Buck] Darling, Pgs. 85, 86
Capt. James A Graham, Pg. 143
Cardinal Dougherty H.S., Pgs. 24, 25, 34
Carlos Castaneda, Pgs. 168, 224
Carpentry school, Pg. 212
Cathy, Pgs. 164, 180
CCP [Corrective Custody Platoon], Pg. 29
Cheltenham, Pa., Pgs. 3, 5, 10, 207
Cheltenham H. S. Pgs. 25,

110, 113
Cherry Hill, N.J., Pg. 16
"CHESTY" Puller, Pgs. 184, 185
"CHIEF" Maybee, Pgs. 40, 41
China, [Kowloon] Pgs. 53, 81
CIA, Pg. 197
Chris [Smigle's corner], Pg. 20
Chu Lia, Vietnam, Pgs. 59, 60, 61, 64, 71, 87, 88, 93, 143
Citation [SILVER STAR], Pgs. 175, 176, 177
Clark A.F.B., Pg. 153
Col. Hilgartner, Pg. 138
Congressmen Jimmy Burns, Pgs. 113, 161
Corfu [Greece] Pg. 47
Cpl. McKinley, Pgs. 60, 122, 123, 129, 130, 131
Cpl. Peterson, Pgs. 119, 120, 121, 144, 145, 153
Cpl. Smith, Pgs. 143, 144, 153
Crete [Mediterranean Sea] Pg. 48

Da Nang [Vietnam], Pgs. 59, 153, 157
Dad, Pgs. 3, 4, 7, 16, 31, 37, 71, 87, 109 thru 113, 134 thru 139
Debbie, Pgs. 219, 221, 225, 227, 228, 237
Delta Company, 1st Battalion, 5th Regiment, 1st Marine Division, Pgs. 60, 61, 113, 119, 141, 155, 156, 176
DI's [Drill Instructors], Pgs. 28 thru 37
Distinguish flying Cross, Pg. 151
Don Juan, Pgs. 168
Door Gunner, Pg.148, 149

DVOP [Disabled Veteran Outreach Program], Pgs. 233, 234

Ed Clark, Pgs. 239, 240

F-4: "Phantom" - attack aircraft, Pg.150
Factory work, Pg. 200
Family Names, pg. 3
Father Bennett, Pg. 34
"Fighting 5th" [Nickname of the 5th Regiment], Pgs. 59, 60
"Fits" [Squad member], Pgs. 124, 151
Fl. St. Employment Service [FSES], Pg. 233

Gatling-gun, Pg. 152
General Wallace M Green, Pgs. 175, 178
Germantown [Philadelphia, Pa.], 201
Gerry Doyle, Pg. 11
GI Bill, Pgs. 112, 189, 202, 204, 215, 216, 217, 225, 231
Good Humor Ice Cream Co., Pgs. 200 thru 202
Guam, Pgs. 159 thru 161

Happy Valley, Pgs. 61 thru 63, 109
Harvey Lake, Pgs.214 thru 216
Harry G Summers Jr., Pg. 2
Hawaii, Pg. 161
Hill 51, pg. 132
Hill 54, pgs. 59, 61, 63, 85, 95 thru 101
Hill 110, Pg. 105
Halloween ritual, Pg.21, 22
Hue City {Vietnam], Pgs. 157

THE BEST OF THE BEST · 247

Huey Helicopter crash incident, Pg.194
Hurricane Hazel, Pg. 11
Hurricane, name unknown, Pg. 51

Iraq, Pgs. 1, 184, 196, 197
Italy, Pgs. 46 thru 48

Jack [Brother], Pgs. 3, 4, 23, 111, 112
Jacksonville, N.C., Pg. 41,
Janis Joplin, Pg. 203
Janet, Pgs. 213 thru 216
Jay, Pg. 237
Jeri, Pg. 27
Jim [Brother], Pgs. 3, 238
Jimmy [Uncle], Pg. 205
John [vet], Pgs. 168, 232
Joe Doyle, Pgs. 170, 171
Joey [Smigle's corner], Pg. 23
John Isley, Pg. 71

Karen [Wife], Pgs. 237 thru 240
Kensington, Phila. Pg. 113
Kowloon [China], Pgs. 53, 81, 138, 139, 147

Lama De Revelino [Italy], Pg.47
La Nag-2, Pg. 103
Lansdale [Philadelphia], Pg. 15
Larry Bayer, Pg. 233, 234
L/Cpl. Santo, Pgs. 144 thru 147, 152, 153
Leaches, Pg. 107
Lebedos Bay [Turkey], Pg. 47
Leather trade, Pg. 211, 212
Lincoln Prep, Pgs. 204, 207
Liz [Sister], Pg. 3, 111
Livorno [Italy], Pg.48

Machamity Creek, Pg. 170
Man Trap, Pg. 114, 115
Mary, Pgs. 199, 203 thru 207
McGuire A.F.B., Pg. 161
Med-Cruise, Pgs. 45 thru 51, 53
Meg [Sister], Pgs. 3, 241
Melrose Academy, Pg. 6
Melrose Country Club, Pg. 12
Mess Duty, Pg. 83 thru 86
Melvin B, Pg. 39
Mike [Brother], Pgs. 3, 6, 112, 135, 221 thru 224, 230, 231, 237
Mike [Cousin], Pgs. 15, 17, 23, 27, 110, 113, 137
Mike Harold, Pg. 240
Miller, Pg. 151
Mimi Ma, Pgs. 81, 113, 136, 138, 139, 236
Mom, Pgs. 3 thru 6, 9, 110, 111, 137, 160, 161
Mrs. M. Haley, Pg. 111
Mrs. M. Jonas, Pg. 111
Naples [Italy], Pgs. 46 thru 48, 54

NATO Troops, Pg. 47
Netanyahu, Pg. 25
News's Stations [ABC, CBS, NBC], Pg. 64
Nun's, Pg. 6
Okinawa, Pg.57
Olivia, Pgs. 1, 2, 109, 198, 235,241
"On Strategy" [Book], Pg. 2
Operations:
  Colorado, Pg. 93
  Swift, Pg. 155
  Union, Pgs. 103 thru 139, 156, 176
  Union II, Pgs. 141 thru 156

Parris Island, S. C. [P.I.], Pgs. 27 thru 38
Penn St. Univ., Pgs. 213 thru 219, 225
Philadelphia, Pa., Pgs. 3, 27, 28 37, 39, 43, 44, 51, 52, 111, 113, 161, 163 thru 181, 201 thru 207, 213
Philadelphia Naval Bass, Pgs. 166, 180, 181, 199
Philadelphia Naval Hospital, Pgs. 161 thru 180
Philippines, Pgs. 153, 159
Pittsburgh, Pa., Pgs. 225, 227, 228, 233
Phoc Duc, Pg. 121, 131
Platoon 123 [P.I.], Pg. 28, 37
Pocono Mountains, Pg. 213
"Point Man", Pgs. 69, 104, 105, 114 thru 116, 119 thru 122, 142
Potomac River incident, Pgs. 193, 194
Propaganda, Pg. 106
Post Traumatic Stress Disorder [PTSD], Pgs. 1, 196
"Puff", Pg. 152
Purple Heart, Pgs. 1, 91, 126, 134, 161, 185
Purple Porpoise Bar, Pg. 240

Quang Nam, Pgs. 103, 156
Quang Ngai, Pg. 60
Quang Tin, Pgs. 103, 156
Quantico [Virginia], Pgs. 183 thru 194
Que Son Mountains, Pgs. 141, 150
Que Son Valley, Pgs. 93, 141

R&R, Pgs. 53, 81, 88
"Red" Chinese, Pg. 106
Redondo Beach [California], Pg. 209

Reggie Jackson, Pg. 25
Rifle Range [Qualification], Pgs. 28 thru 34
Rope Swing incident, Pgs. 170, 171
Rota [Spain], Pg. 46
Roxanne, Pg. 16
Russ [Smigle's corner], Pg 20

Sandoval – APA 54 [U.S. Naval Ship], Pg.45
Santa Fe Community College [SFCC], Pgs. 225, 229, 231
Sanuchi, Pg. 46
Sardinia [Mediterranean], Pg. 48
SGT. Holler, Pg. 60
Shawn [Son], Pgs. 238, 239
"Shit Bird", Pg. 91, 92, 104
Silver Star, Pgs. 1, 138, 175 thru 178, 185
Sister Nalla, Pg. 6, 7
Smigle's Corner, Pgs. 15, 19, 20, 71, 165, 199, 203
Sniper, Pg. 190
Song Chang River, Pg. 115
Spain, Pgs. 46, 48, 49
South China Sea, Pg. 61
South Korean Marines, Pgs.71, 73, 88, 89
Steve [Brother], Pg. 3
Steve McQueen, Pgs.179,180
St. Joseph's Grade School, Pgs.5, 11
Subic Bay [Philippines], Pgs. 153, 159
Sue [Sister], Pgs. 3, 110, 212

Tam Ky, Pgs. 101,109, 141, 153
Tet [67], Pg. 71

THE BEST OF THE BEST • 249

Tet [68], Pg.157, 184
Timbakion [Crete], Pg. 48
Tom [Brother], Pgs. 3, 4, 112
Tommy J. [High School], Pg. 24
Tookany Creek, Park, Parkway: Pgs. 11 thru 13
Trapping [Muskrat], Pg. 10
Trenton [New Jersey], Pg. 201
Trieste [Italy], Pg. 47
"Tunnel Rat", Pgs. 13, 77; 78, 105, 142
Turkey [Mediterranean Sea], Pg. 47, 48

USNS Barrett, Pgs. 53 thru 57
USNA [US Naval Academy], Pg. 238
USPS, Pgs. 168, 235, 238, 241, 244

VA Hospital, Pgs. 2, 221
Venatolia, Pg. 46
Virginia [State], Pg. 183
Vine Hay Village, Pg. 141
Washington, DC, Pgs.183, 188, 190

Water Buffalo Incident, Pg. 79
Watkins Glen and Woodstock Concerts: Pg. 203, 204
Wildwood [N.J.], Pg. 15 thru 17, 60

Yaqui [Native American Indians], Pg. 168, 224

CPSIA information can be obtained at www.ICGtesting.com
Printed in the USA
LVOW060050251011

251902LV00001B/16/P